Keep Halloween weird!

SEXY LEPER

X-ender

CHAD STROUP

Bizarro Pulp Press
an imprint of JournalStone Publishing

Bizarro Pulp Press books may be ordered through booksellers or by contacting:

Bizarro Pulp Press, a JournalStone imprint
   www.BizarroPulpPress.com

   Print ISBN: 978-1-947654-83-9
   Ebook ISBN: 978-1-947654-84-6

Printed in the United States of America
JournalStone rev. date: March 22, 2019

Cover Art: D.F. Noble

Interior Formatting: Lori Michelle
   www.theauthorsalley.com

Edited by: Vincenzo Bilof

CHAPTER ONE

BEFORE THIS AFTERNOON, Kat Dyer had never stroked a dinosaur's back before. She supposed there was a first time for everything, though, and she convinced herself the material she was touching had to have been borrowed from the preserved, flayed flesh of some big extinct lizard. The raw, scaly texture chafed the tips of her fingers. It was mapped with patches of burgundy hues. Bubbles and pustules and indeterminate formations. Kat felt like she was going to need an extreme lotion bath after the reluctant caress.

On the wall beside her, deflated rubber faces hung from hooks, waiting to be filled and be given some semblance of life. A pale, beautifully dead woman with electrocuted black hair, a shock of white wriggling up from each temple. A demonic visage that was somehow part clown and part Jack-O'-Lantern. A former president, but Kat was not exactly sure which one. A face that looked as if it had been constructed completely out of expired bologna. And a ghostly, expressionless shape that for some reason reminded her of the main actor from that boring old sci-fi TV show Jack always raved about.

"Um, well," Kat said, her sparkling pink bottom lip wetting the curve of her top lip, "I guess this is kinda, uh, neat in a weird way, but would it be cool if I got my real costume now? Please? I'm, like, kind of in a hurry and I still need to go home and get ready."

The clerk behind the counter chewed the corners of his thumb.

The line behind Kat was almost out the door, but she wasn't budging until this issue was sorted out. He was going to have to satisfy her or risk pissing off a dozen desperate customers.

Screw the other customers. He was going to have to risk pissing *her* off.

His nametag read: MAHBOOB, which made Kat snicker inside. She'd have to remember that one and laugh about it with Jack later. What kind of a name was that, anyway? What kind of a mother would let that slide?

Mahboob's eyebrows blended into one, resembling an ungroomed and misplaced handlebar mustache. His pebbly eyes refused to quaver. His other hand—the one that was not being self-cannibalized—seemed to work of its own volition, slamming a price gun atop a row of prepackaged stage makeup and vampire fangs. Kat worried that the force of his blows would shatter the glass below. She couldn't afford to get cut by some wayward shards.

The faux-vintage jewelry enclosed in the case looked surprisingly real. A blinking sign above Mahboob's head read: COSMO'S CUSTOM COSTUMES. Behind him, rows and rows of the thinnest thread and the thickest yarn of all colors and sizes, arranged in a way that likely only made sense to the employees. Next to the yarn were various shades of lipstick, from fuchsia to utter darkness. Wigs hung on blank Styrofoam heads, scalped from some unsuspecting victim and placed atop a face that could not scream. There were plastic tubs stacked behind the counter, so low that Kat could barely see them, with homemade labels that said GUNS and KNIVES. She absently spun the sunglasses rack next to her and saw a glittery silver pair she would have considered buying if she had extra money. She was already late on rent, so even next payday wasn't exactly going to multiply the zeros in her bank account.

She was already regretting the decision of pinching her pennies to get this costume made, especially since they screwed it up royally.

"No," Mahboob said. "Is definitely yours."

With one hand, Kat held the disgusting, lumpy costume out toward Mahboob, wincing as if the limp weight were a rotting fish. She twirled the tip of her blonde bob with her other hand, forming the short strands into a spiral. "I'm sorry . . . there must be some sort of mistake. This belongs to someone else. Not me. My name is Kat . . . Kat Dyer? Can you double-check please?"

Mahboob grumbled, waved at the antsy customers behind Kat as if to express it would only take a moment, and reached underneath the costume's sequin-plagued dress with a gesture that most passersby would have considered molestation. He held up one finger to Kat, then skipped to the back of the store to some far off corridor that could not possibly fit within the square footage of the building. Kat could barely see him pull a small rope, which turned on a swinging, uncovered light bulb. He inspected the private region of the costume like a novice gynecologist, then returned to the front counter, pulled out a flimsy manila tag from within, and waved it in Kat's face. His fingernails were impossibly immaculate. Any grime that might have once inhabited their crevices had been meticulously eradicated. He tapped the tag impatiently. Kat's name and current phone number were clearly visible.

"I really don't understand . . . this isn't what I ordered." Frustrated tears dampened the corners of Kat's eyes. She bent her knee, rested her foot flat on the tree behind her.

The English walnut tree planted smack dab in the center of the costume shop.

Its trunk was as thick as a mammoth's leg, and a crude shape had been cut out of the ceiling to allow the tree space to reach toward the sky. Birds hopped in the highest branches, and a line of black ants paused in a forced end to their march, stuck in the leaking sap. The unique ecosystem survived even though it had absolutely no right to exist within the walls of a costume shop.

Mahboob yawned wide enough for a bear to crawl in and hibernate. He wet his finger, flipped through the pages of a tiny organizer, and showed Kat that the number on the tag coincided with the original order. "Yes," he said. "Is correct. Is unconventional choice, but we aim to please! No request too extreme. When we no have costume in stock, we craft by the hand whatever your mind desire. Very special limited edition. One of a kind. Materials most secret." Mahboob grinned. His teeth were at the opposite end of the spectrum from his fingernails. They looked like white galoshes that had spent too much time splashing in a day-old puddle.

"But my mind *desired* a sexy leopard costume, not whatever the hell this is."

"Sexy *what* you say, now?" Mahboob raised his left eyebrow, the right side tagging along because it didn't really have a choice.

"Leopard. *Leopard.*"

"What is lippard?"

"You know, like a big, fast cat with spots. Cat, like my name, but with a 'c' instead of a 'k.' Rawr." Kat pawed playfully in the air at Mahboob, trying to withhold her vexation and failing miserably. Mahboob's eyes seemed incapable of blinking. They glazed over as he lost himself in deep thought. He scratched at a raisin-sized mole on his nose and for just a second it seemed like it might detach. Kat could hear his lungs exchanging carbon dioxide for oxygen. "But it's like a cute, sexy person version, you know? Like, it looks like you more or less got the dress right, so kudos for that, I guess, but this doesn't look anything like a leopard to me. This doesn't even look like the picture in your catalog."

The woman immediately behind Kat was growing restless. "Are you almost done here?" she asked. Her face was a shiny red apple. "This is ridiculous. I need to pick up my kids in thirty minutes."

Kat shot the woman a well-practiced stink eye. Before the woman had a chance to respond, a tall man with a shaved head and a goatee the size and shape of a skunk's tail approached them.

"Ma'am," he said to the red-faced woman, "I can help you at the next register."

"Well, thank God for that," the woman replied, storming off to an adjacent counter. A few other impatient customers split from Kat's line and followed the red-faced woman.

March, lemmings, march, Kat thought.

She could feel a burning stare coming from the goateed man's eyes. A typically lustful gaze that she was more than used to, had always been used to, would never truly be used to. Unwanted attention: the bane of any woman's existence. She did not acknowledge it, and the employee took the hint and dashed off to do damage control on the angry mom.

"Oh my, oh dear," Mahboob said. "This is not good. Who you speak to with?" His concern sounded staged, though it also sounded like he'd had some recent practice with the act. She knew this well.

The daily life of working in retail hell, where the customer was always right even when they couldn't have been more wrong.

But that wasn't her. Not now. She knew better than to be *that* customer.

"I don't know. A woman. She sounded kinda old."

"Oh nonononono. I tell Cosmo that Maa should never be taking the order. She deaf in one ear." Mahboob grabbed his left ear and squeezed it, made it open and close like a sock puppet's mouth.

"So you're saying I ended up with whatever the hell *this* is because your mother heard me wrong? I don't—"

"I say nothing of the sort. This what you order." He waved the tag in Kat's face again as if it were notice of a recently passed law.

"No it isn't. You just said—Seriously, what *is* this? It's gross. I knew I shouldn't have paid up front. I'd really like my money back, please." The arches of Kat's feet stretched and flattened. Her elbows popped and flexed. She breathed slowly, deeply.

"No returns." Mahboob jabbed his gargantuan finger in the direction of a tin sign that said exactly those two words. "Is store policy. Around Maa, you need emaciate."

"I need what?"

"You need speaking clearly. Sorry, but there is nothing I can do for you." Mahboob folded his arms into a hairy infinity symbol.

"But . . . but tonight's Halloween. I don't have any other options."

Mahboob reached beneath the counter without so much as glancing sideways, whipped out a catalog the size of a phonebook, turned to a random page, and shoved it in Kat's face. "Perhaps I interest you in this Raggedy Ann or pregnant nun costume? Both in stock. Special discount for new customer! You want me to go get?"

"I can't afford to buy another one. And, to be perfectly honest, I shouldn't have to. Can't I just exchange this one?"

"You already met my good friend No Returns. Now meeting his brother No Exchanges." Mahboob wiggled his finger at another tin sign stating these words, the same color and general shape as the first sign. Kat wondered why the two sentiments could not have been combined into one all-purpose sign.

There was now a man directly behind Kat. She had already heard him shifting impatiently, but now she could almost smell his frustration.

"Jesus, lady," the man said. "Come on! Some of us have places to be!"

"Ugh . . . fine!" Kat snatched the costume back from Mahboob and draped it over her shoulders like a mink stole. She ignored the itching sensation and stormed out of Cosmo's Custom Costumes, somehow managing to dodge every warm body in her way. A good thing, since she wasn't in an apologetic mood. Her marching tantrum was still audible after she closed the front door and stampeded through the parking lot, straight toward her car.

She kept her head down as she mumbled incoherent obscenities and crashed face-first into a pole. She yelped, partially out of fright, partially due to shocking pain, and when she lifted her face she saw that it wasn't a pole after all.

It was Jack.

She almost peed herself at the sight of him. Embarrassment, delight, some strange mixture of the two.

"Hey Kitty Kat," he said, lightly grabbing her arm to steady her. "Better watch where you're goin'. What's crackin'?"

"Don't call me that, Jack." She was completely fine with being called that.

"That your costume?"

Kat whipped the costume away from her neck, clutched the wretched, meaty fabric to her body, and blocked it with her too-small purse.

"Um . . . maybe. Not ready for human eyes yet. Gonna have to wait until the party."

"Not even for me? Sooooo secretive." Jack's dark eyes darted back and forth behind his thick, black-rimmed glasses. His hair was huge and coiffed, somehow defying gravity despite having next to zero product in it. The slight wind momentarily blew it to one side before it bounced perfectly back into place. His lime green shirt proclaimed: "I'M WITH STUPID," complete with a thick arrow pointing toward his own head.

"Especially not for you, jerk face." Kat stuck out her tongue, her mood shifting from angry to flirty. "You getting your costume at this shit shack, too? Better watch out for asshole face working the counter. Which, by the way, when we talk later I wanna know how hard it was to hold in your laughter after seeing his name. I mean, wow."

"Nah . . . I'm just popping into the Goodwill. Gonna grab some pants I can tear up real good for tonight."

"Oh, cause, like, you can only afford the discount stuff."

"Hey, you can't take the 'bargain' out of 'bargain hunter,' or something like that. To be honest, though, my dad says 'no job, no trust fund access.' Kinda sucks, but whatever."

"Why don't you just go back and finish up your stylist credentials? You were doing so well at the hair academy. You know you won't have any problem getting a chair at a good salon."

Jack shrugged. "Eh. I don't know if my heart's completely in it yet. I think I need to find myself first. See the world. That's what everyone says you're supposed to do at our age, right?"

"You do realize people still need A-line cuts, faux hawks, and weaves on the other side of the globe, right?"

"Speaking of which," Jack said as he squeezed a small chunk of her hair, "you're about due for another cut. Maybe trim your bangs at least."

"Stop deflecting."

"Yeah, yeah, okay. I hear ya. My inner quest can wait. I need to find a loophole to access my trust first anyway."

"Hey, so what are you going as tonight?"

"Can't tell you. I'd have to kill you."

"Oh, God. You're not going as the Wolf Man again, are you?"

"Um . . . no? Maybe, maybe not. Hey, when I like something and it works, I stick with it. It's why I still hang around you." Jack offered an exaggerated wink and lightly knocked his knuckles on Kat's shoulder. Kat groaned at the far-too-familiar joke, one she had heard for too many years to count, even though deep down she was flattered by it. And she also knew there was a certain level of earnestness floating just below the funny. Jack's truths always came wrapped tightly in humor.

"Okay, I've really gotta motor so I can get ready for tonight. See ya, hon." She kissed Jack on his dimpled cheek, felt a tickle on her lips from his ever-present five o'clock shadow, and skipped away like a schoolgirl. Even though Kat did not have eyes in the back of her head, she knew he was watching her make it to her car safely. Jack was reliable that way. A bodyguard she didn't have to pay. A boyfriend she didn't have to screw.

Kat wondered why Jack hadn't returned any of her phone calls for over a week. Their friendship had always been at least a "talk every other night" sort of bond, one that always seemed on the verge of morphing the word "friend" into "relation," but backed out at the last second because it might have been a little weird. But guys often got busy with things that didn't concern girls. Just the way the world worked. It wasn't like she didn't have her own life. Still, she was hurt by the situation, but she decided not to bring it up. Yet. Maybe at the party, where there would be safety in numbers. Where the wrong words might be lost in the cacophony of party conversation.

She twisted the key, turned the radio up to 11, rolled down the window halfway because that was as far as it would go anymore, drove away from the decrepit strip mall, and headed west on Ventura Boulevard, passing endless smoke shops, liquor stores, and Chinese takeout restaurants over and over and over as if she were trapped in a cheap commerce loop.

CHAPTER TWO

I T HUNG. Like a victim on a meat hook. Like the remnant of a once lively soul left to dry, crack, and heal like fine venison jerky.

It hung on the outside of the closet door, begging for life it never had, never could have had. Its limp form was an intruder in the reflection of Kat's vanity mirror. Kat tried to shift her head enough to block it, but it ended up being too difficult to do her makeup so she gave in.

A warm breeze pushed through her open window, causing the costume to dance as if it were enjoying the raucous sounds that were booming from KROQ on the stereo next door. The rotten husk almost seemed to whisper to her that it needed to be filled with her mind, her body, her soul.

Kat spun her chair around and faced the costume. She unwittingly took the glove in her hand and rubbed it with her untarnished fingers. Within seconds the chafing became almost unbearable and she felt the need to dip her hand in a jar of lavender lotion and soak it overnight. The scent of the leathery latex was familiar and somehow comforting, like a new friend imitating an old friend.

Join me, it seemed to be saying. Join me. Know me. Become me.

Kat turned back to the mirror, ignoring the fabricated calling. She was getting way too good at freaking herself out. The games she had played with herself when she was a child—the ghost stories she had made up and shared with only her most treasured teddy bears and Barbie dolls were now coming back to haunt her. But it was Halloween, so she figured she had to do something to give herself the shivers.

And her costume was certainly making the task easy.

A set of photo booth pictures was wedged into the corner of the mirror. Some of her most cherished moments with her closest friends. Her and Jack, making goofy faces, trying on absurd mustaches and hats. A single shot of Hannah hugging Kat on Graduation Day at Ulysses S. Grant (Hannah went to Harvard-Westlake, the lucky bitch). Perfect memories trapped in chemically treated paper.

She blocked out the sounds—both inside and outside—and focused on her makeup. Black charcoal eyes. Pale, nude, dead cheeks. Halloween was here. Here to stay.

———— • ♦ • ————

Nearly an hour later, Kat was reluctantly dressed for the imminent party. She slumped in front of the mirror and took a deep breath before lifting her eyes. The horrifying reflection made her hop from one foot to the other. She was her own haunted house jump scare. She could not bear to scrutinize herself while stepping into the outfit, only using minor candlelight and the power of denial to aid in her preparation, but now—with the blinding light of her uncovered lamp forcing her to see—she paused for a few seconds to finally absorb her completed look.

For someone who hated horror films, refused to even watch trailers for them, was pushed nearly to the point of nausea just by the thought of them, she had managed to transform into a living, breathing version of a low-budget 70s schlockfest.

Latex legs hugged her like previously used tights, plastic pustules were strategically placed on the material, giving off the impression that she had been wading in boiled oil. The seams at the bottom were hidden by mid-leg suede boots complete with three-inch heels. Her own addition, not courtesy of Cosmo's. The costume's material was sewn into a white dress cut more than a few inches above the knee, a dress that fit her body like a prophylactic, covering her entire torso aside from the tip of her now mutated cleavage. Arms that looked like a bird's eye view of Mount Everest fit like leather evening gloves.

She sniffed near her elbow and wondered if it was her or the costume that smelled like a Slim Jim. Kat turned her face so her natural unblemished side filled the mirror, hoping to obscure the monstrosity she was allowing herself to impersonate, and blinked with big fake lashes that would make Betty Boop blush.

Even at this angle, she couldn't force the illusion.

Her lips looked startlingly out of place, like she had just finished sucking down a smoothie made of pureed glitter. Her blonde bob was sharp and styled, sprayed to weapon-like precision. She turned back the other direction and almost urinated at the sight. A seamless connection from her bosom traveled around her throat and covered the left half of her face. The attachment made her cheek droop with boils and growths that begged to be burst. She hadn't even needed to apply spirit gum to keep the prosthetics firmly attached. Despite her ill feelings toward the whole situation, Kat could not deny the quality of the costume. There was something to be said for expert craftsmanship, for stark realism in dark and twisted imagination.

She checked her alarm clock. Time to go. She didn't want to go. She had to go. She shouldn't go. But Hannah would never let her hear the end of it if she didn't at least make an appearance. And Hannah already was the type to never shut up, no matter if the commentary was referencing occupying Beverly Blvd., the state of Sarah Palin's wardrobe, or the organic tuna salad she had for lunch. And which would be worse—showing up only to revolt the crowd or not showing up and being forgotten by the masses?

She'd just go for an hour, hang out with Hannah and Jack for a while, have a few drinks, then feign illness. Quick and relatively painless. The way she looked, it wouldn't take much of an act for anyone to believe her.

She wondered if Jack would finally try to make a move on her tonight. She saw it in his eyes in the parking lot, knew he wanted to, but he was still being some sort of polite gentleman so as not to offend her or something. Kat was not sure if this made her care even more about him or just outright loathe him. She decided she was not going to bother caring. No guy with half his eyesight or a quarter of his mental faculties was going to look at her with any affection tonight. Not a vato with facial tattoos, a beach punk with a purple cock ring, a (barely) former teacher, a chubby Korean with slight man boobs. Despite being Kat's actual real life sexual checklist, the list seemed more and more cartoonish as it went on in her head. Her sex life was a sick routine, but it was the only one she knew, so she was going to have to stick with it. She'd have to wait for another night to screw someone else who wasn't Jack and who would forget to call her the following morning.

And eventually she'd have Jack. That's the way things were supposed to work. Patience and persistence. In the meantime, she'd practice. She'd make perfect.

She grabbed her tiny purse, so small it might as well have belonged to a Cabbage Patch Kid, and left.

Kat stepped out of her apartment building onto the corner of Victory and Kester. It was a humid night, the autumn climate bathing in the aftermath of Santa Ana winds. She was thankful that the streets appeared deserted, and she could almost picture her body hidden in the safety of her beat-to-hell blood red '78 Beetle. Though it was only parked a few blocks away, it seemed so unfathomably far. Each step she took was daunting. She was an ant attempting to cross a kitchen floor. She occasionally paused to shove her body into a shadowed doorjamb of another building, then looked both ways and leaped back into the street. She breathed comfortably. She was safe. It was far too late for any trick-or-treating-stragglers.

Except it wasn't.

Impish laughter echoed behind her, caused her fine arm hairs to harden and her heart to sink. The weird flesh of her costume seemed to grow cold against her own skin, which was oddly refreshing, and she turned to investigate the playful sounds. She entered the light beam burning from a street lamp and saw a tiny curly-haired Hispanic girl dressed as some indeterminate Disney princess. The little girl screamed as if she had just seen an honest-to-God monster and immediately headed in the opposite direction, probably in search of the nearest torch or stone or the angry mob that could supply these tools. Then she saw a young boy dressed as a cowboy who was presumably accompanying the princess. Was he the little girl's brother, her pre-pubescent "boyfriend" who wouldn't hold her hand for all the Willy Wonka candy in the world? Kat could not say. She wasn't even sure how old he was. What did she know about kids?

The boy stood bowlegged, as if parodying his own costume,

waiting for a post-sunset showdown. His left hand clasped a plastic toy gun and his right hovered near his back pocket. He did not seem the least bit phased by the strange sight in front of him. He stared at Kat, his eyes like cold, smooth stone.

"Put 'em up," the boy said, waving the orange gun in Kat's direction. She temporarily ignored her own freakishness, was almost able to forget about it for the time being, and played along, even adding a small "eek" for full effect. The boy pointed his gun toward the sky and pulled the trigger. The jarring pop made Kat's body involuntarily jerk, and she thought she might have urinated just a bit, but then the combination of reason and the small puff of smoke leaking from the weapon informed her that it was just a harmless cap gun. No cause for alarm. "Okay, so trick or treat now," the cowboy continued. "Gimme some goddamn candy, sweet tits."

Kat audibly gasped and wrapped her arms around her chest, and she was not sure if she should be offended or flattered. She wondered if this boy was even old enough to know the difference between attractive and revolting, and if he would one day realize there was sometimes a fine line between the two. At his prepubescent age, it was entirely possible that the lines were blurred.

"Maybe you should have been a sailor instead, little guy," she said, trying to balance authority with gaiety. "You sure have a mouth like one. Sorry, no candy tonight. Party calls. Gotta motor."

"Trick it is, then, lil' darlin'," the mini-cowboy said, not even flinching as he whipped his right hand forward, releasing an egg. It soared through the air so quickly that Kat barely had a chance to register what it was, much less dodge it. It smashed against Kat's hip. She screamed and looked down at the yolky mucous oozing down her side.

"Huevos de puta!" the boy yelled.

By the time Kat looked back up, the tiny cowboy had vanished. Indiscernible child shrieks echoed from around the corner, bouncing from building to building. A car full of teenagers peeled down the street, the passengers screaming with unbridled excitement. Kat decided she might have a horrible costume, but that it was going to be a clean one, dammit, and headed back up to her apartment to ensure that would be the case.

She completed this task in record time and returned to the street, repeating her hiding ritual before finally reaching her car, only to find it completely wrapped in toilet paper. The Mummy-Mobile, reporting for duty. Someone actually took the time to drape the toilet paper beneath the car on each pass. Impressive. Still, knowing this neighborhood, it could have been worse. God, how she hated kids, even though she was barely old enough to be considered an adult. According to her parents, this was a topic still up for debate, despite the fact she had held onto a job at Benji's Boutique for six months and had maintained her own apartment without the need for a roommate. In a shitty part of Van Nuys, but still . . . it was better than nothing.

After removing the majority of the toilet paper, she got in and turned the key. The stereo vomited out sounds that might have actually been created by hogs rather than humans, and she switched the dial to an oldies station. She let the Beetle warm up for a minute, waited until it purred softly, then shifted into first gear.

She did not acknowledge the beige Pacer X parked behind her, nor did she notice the fuzzy blue face behind its wheel, nor did she realize that this car pulled out of its spot mere seconds after she zipped away from hers. Following her closely, yet casually. At a safe distance.

CHAPTER THREE

T HE HILLS.

The Hollywood Hills have always been a sinuous mess, a conundrum within a puzzle within a nightmarish headache, twisting and turning through neighborhoods Kat should reasonably have known by heart by now. But now they felt fresh and new, like they had shifted since the last time she buzzed along these streets. Streets so tight and narrow that sometimes accidentally led into driveways or dead ends. Untrimmed Amazonian palm trees, their leaves beckoning to any who might look, their shadows beneath the streetlights forming dark, gigantic talons that scraped across the road.

Bentleys and Porsches and BMWs zipped by in the opposite direction, their un-costumed drivers on their way to God-Knows-Where. Her Beetle bitched and moaned and climbed and Kat wished she had stayed in the Valley. Here, in the hills, Kat would always be the fish that yearned to be in a much larger and deeper pond, relatively safe from the predatory claws of thieving raccoons.

The hills, the hell.

———— ◆ ————

Kat was what some might refer to as "downright pretty." In the prime of her callow life at twenty-two, she boasted a slender figure that did not require intensive dieting, faux-Asian eyes that resulted in constant racial misunderstandings despite her natural blonde hair, small and perky breasts that could potentially melt in any man's hands if granted the chance to give them a squeeze, contoured cheekbones that were hollowed out by God's spoon.

She had grown accustomed to leers of lust in recent years, had even welcomed them on certain occasions, only from young men lacking any obvious deformities, if not preposterous quirks. She wished at least a few of these stares came from Jack, but she honestly couldn't figure out why. Still, an ego boost could do wonders for a girl's complexion, and sometimes the lonelies allowed lust to be enough. Tonight was different. Kat wished she could will herself invisible, but ultimately that would defeat the purpose of showing up in the first place.

She needed to be seen, but at the same time hoped the majority of the partygoers were too high to notice her. Most likely, the latter would be the case, but she was damned either way.

The double doors to Hannah Harper's house were unlocked for both guests and crashers. You threw a party in the hills, there was no telling who the hell might show up. For some, the whole point of opening their homes to friends was to increase the chances of allowing strangers to stroll their floors. A party wasn't worth throwing or attending if it lacked an element of danger.

Kat entered into the cobwebbed catacombs of the party-in-progress, and immediately the expressions of lust she'd expected were closer to raw abhorrence. The scents of building sweat and spilling alcohol and moldy Mary Jane mixed and thickened the atmosphere. Bottles of liquor brands she had never even heard of sparkled beneath the recessed lighting. A sea of costumes ebbed and flowed in a twisted Halloween dream. Zombie Construction Worker. Dracula in Drag. Osama Ben Franklin. Baby Doll Buttcheeks. Castrated Flasher. Dinosaur Head. Slutty Jesus.

The stereo system blasted some trendy Autotuned artist that Kat publicly eschewed yet secretly adored. She drifted through the long, narrow hallways, passing by dilated pupils and patches of overdone cologne. Buzzed bodies gyrated with questionable rhythm, grinding against one another like elements of erosion. Those who bothered to notice Kat cowered away in absurd terror from the wet-dream-gone-sickening-nightmare before them. They could not begin to fathom what her choice of costume was. They were too terrified to ask. Kat was thankful to avoid the confrontation. She wouldn't have had a reasonable answer anyway.

She moved on, focused forward. Red plastic cups became beacons to the alcohol supply she so badly needed to locate so she could begin forgetting this night already.

She decided to seek out Hannah, hoping her BFF would be able to offer support in this time of need. Before Kat began her search, she paused at a sparkling crystal bowl filled with candy corn and reached in for a handful, despite the fact she was supposed to be on a strict diet of kale, cucumber, green apple smoothies.

Screw it, Kat thought. *Diets are a joke. They're for people who have no life. Which I guess is more or less me, but still . . .*

Though she was not sure how she was able to feel anything through her faux fingers, she immediately noticed something was wrong—the candy corn appeared to have magically melted, even though it was not particularly warm inside the house. She immediately tossed back the few mushy pieces she grabbed, but the waxy colors had already painted the world's shittiest rainbow across her protected palm. She looked in both directions before licking the sticky goo away. She'd consumed worse in front of a more attentive crowd. At least the flavor was still intact, which reminded her she really didn't care much for candy corn.

Kat continued weaving her way through the crowd until she found what she needed most: a punch bowl filled with an indeterminate adult beverage sitting atop a table made of Carpathian elm. She took a few steps in the imagined right direction before slamming face-first into a giant blue fox. It looked like something that just came from a furry convention. Which, knowing this crowd, was entirely possible. Deviancy was only one of many layers of pleasure up here in the hills.

Kat tried to peer into the fox's eyeholes, which were adorned with exploding eyelashes that somehow sidestepped effeminacy. "Who is that in there?" she asked. "Do I know you?" Between the headache-inducing music and the distortion factor caused by the mask, the response was reduced mostly to mumbles, though she was ninety-nine percent certain she heard the name "Jack" in there.

The fox-that-was-apparently-Jack handed her an already full cup and, though she really wanted to send the entire beverage on a ride down Throat Mountain, she instead sipped the room temperature drink silently. It tasted strange, as if it were unnecessarily spiked with additional fermented something-or-other. Not a huge surprise. Probably some weird aphrodisiac Hannah requested specifically for tonight. Kat loved and loathed the taste equally.

Jack reached toward the table and handed her some indeterminate finger food. It was grey, soft yet crispy, finger-shaped. She held it and decided she would probably not eat something she couldn't name. She'd have to find a napkin and toss it in the trash later.

Kat's heart sank. She knew Jack would be here, *wanted* him to be here even, at least before this afternoon, but after getting stuck with this train wreck of a costume she wished he had eaten some bad medjool dates and stayed home sick, watched some *7th Heaven* reruns or played some *Super Mario Kart*. He was wheezing heavily behind that blue fox head, so a sick night was still a distinct possibility, though the initial visual damage of her costume had already been done. Still, she was impressed Jack did not show up as the Wolf Man this year. Maybe he was maturing after all, though the maturity level of the replacement costume was questionable at best. She hoped this wouldn't become his new regular choice. He really didn't need to hide his sweet face.

Jack danced with her. Or, more accurately, danced *at* her. She wondered what part of her body language provoked this. This was so unlike him, even after a few drinks. He placed a puffy paw around the small of her back and drew her closer to him. The motion was not aggressive. In fact, it was arguably a gentle gesture, one that made her tingle with desire. However, it was not exactly comfortable to be pulled this close to his furry costume, especially considering the nonexistent comfort of her own outfit. The fur felt like a heated rug. Kat couldn't help but wonder about the pressure near Jack's pocket that felt like a petrified pickle. She hoped it was just a cellphone or a tube of mints, but also kind of hoped it wasn't.

"Mumble mumble, Kat," Jack said, at least that's what Kat thought it sounded like. "Get mumble groove on, mumble." His voice sounded rougher than usual. He pulled away from Kat and threw his arms into the air as if to praise the heavens. After a few moments of foxtrot worship, he brought his arms down, balled his hands, and churned butter with a rhythm that implied he was listening to a completely different song than the one playing. Kat had never seen Jack act this way before, but she'd also never seen him completely smashed before, which she presumed to be the case. Alcohol: the ultimate lubricant for the soul. She shuddered to think of how many drinks Jack must have already consumed to loosen up to this degree. Or what would happen if he moved on to blow.

Kat spent most of her pre-pubescent and adolescent life living next door to Jack. They were forced into a chance friendship that somehow never found the opportunity to fizzle away. In grammar school, Jack had been notorious for stealing Kat's Barbie dolls and melting their faces into mush. To be fair, he did the same thing to his own Ninja Turtles and G.I. Joes. Now, he was capable of performing quadratic equations in his sleep, and so he was Kat's personally chosen algebra tutor. He was also her almost lover. In her mind, at least. They'd only ever kissed once, and that grand event was based on a dare back when they were both fifteen and green. The awkward forced kiss had been oh-so-nice and the following sexual tension between the two of them had grown exponentially over the years and neither of them had ever managed to keep a serious significant other for more than a couple of months despite trying desperately to turn their latest faceless fucks into something meaningful, so their kiss must have meant something.

But now Jack was a dancing blue fox, grunting like a middle-aged man after missionary sex, so Kat chose to take the possible relationship decision a few steps backward. Not that it mattered. Relationships in the mind were nothing more than romantic fiction. Just slap her face on a paperback book cover with a naked Fabio behind her and be done with it.

Kat swayed like a bobble head attached to a dashboard. She was not much of a dancer. She could barely take two steps down the street without tripping on a crack or bumping into another pedestrian. She felt like everyone was looking at them. Probably, *definitely* because they were. Set to puke all over each other and start some vomitus chain reaction all because of a botched costume. Kat couldn't blame them for enjoying the spectacle, though. Not one bit.

She would do the same if the manufactured disease was not attached to her. Hers would be the loudest laughter.

A slower jam with lyrics about sexual apologies oozed from unseen speakers. Neither of them knew how to proceed. Jack, or rather his giant blue fox face, just stared as if awaiting a command. Not a mumble or a motion. Just more intense breathing—the kind that might be on the giving end of an obscene phone call. Kat politely excused herself from Jack, despite the fact that all she wanted to do deep down was unzip his costume and create temporary tattoos across his back with her fingernails. Desire was a cruel bitch. Regardless, this was not the time nor place for such an impulsive act. She did not want to make him gag after long exposure to grotesqueries. She needed to find Hannah, make her appearance and be gone. She promised to find him sooner rather than later and set off through the winding web of partygoers before he had the chance to protest.

CHAPTER FOUR

"I MEAN, IF you want me to be perfectly honest, I'd fuck you," Lucas Lane said matter-of-factly to his brother Carey. His manicured fingernail scratched at his lip, as if calling attention to the pathetic, malformed mustache he had grown just for tonight. Peach fuzz that would have failed to impress any woman with half her eyesight intact. He was in mid-snort, a line of coke across his knife, a replica that accompanied his costume.

Carey's boyfriend Wade cocked his head and released his hand from what was probably a loving grip. There was a brief silence in their circle, insignificant among the loud music and banal conversation coming from the other groups of people surrounding them.

"Definitely," Lucas continued. "I mean . . . not *really*, but you know what I mean."

"So sad that I understand LucasSpeak all too well now after so many years of trying to decipher it and failing," Carey said, adjusting his B-cup falsies so they remained level and looked relatively natural. His drag was near perfect. A dark, shoulder-length wig with purple highlights, just the right amount of makeup that had taken just the right amount of time to apply, a jet-black tulle knee-high party dress with sequined bodice, two-inch black stilettos, legs shaved to smooth perfection, and perfectly matching accessories adorning his arms, neck, and ears, twinkling in the bright party lights. Carey couldn't blame his brother for his crude comments. He looked damned good. He would fuck himself. If he were of that proclivity. "But I totally get it now. It's like Morse code for the socially inept."

"Eh . . . whatever. You never liked Dad's sense of humor either."

"And I can only get down on my knees and thank God for that."

"That's what she sa—"

"Please. Spare us all."

Lucas shrugged. He finished off his ski slope, then released a sigh of relief.

Wade seemed to be pretending he didn't know his almost-brother-in-law. He had to put up with so much to be in Carey's life, and Lucas was one of the biggest problems, but Carey was proud of his beau for pasting on a happy face when in the same room as Lucas. Wade was like a linebacker next to Carey's cheerleader size. He wore the pants in their relationship, in more ways than one, and Carey was perfectly comfortable with that arrangement. Wade was dressed in a homemade Mr. Peanut outfit, but its sub-par craftsmanship made it seem closer to Mr. Penis, a dick with a top hat and monocle. Wade fancied himself a fashion designer, but Carey felt his man had a long way to go before he would be even a blip on Tim Gunn's radar. His large size made the outfit even more ill-advised.

"I don't know why you had to buy that slutty outfit at that hellhole on Ventura," Wade said, his voice as butch as a shirtless lumberjack. "You could have gotten something cheaper elsewhere."

"No way, babe," Carey said. "This dress and wig are *custom*. So much better than some fucking Party City crap. What good is having money if you're never allowed to spend it? You're just jealous I make a hotter chick than you ever could." He sipped his drink with a straw, presumably to avoid smearing his precious black cherry lipstick.

"Trust me, honey. I'm more than okay with my steadfast manliness." Wade was probably hurt by not being given the chance to create Carey's outfit, but ultimately Carey didn't care because looking good on Halloween took precedence over sore feelings that would fade away within a day or two. A neck massage, a hell of a blow job, and Wade would forget all about his hurt feelings.

Wade turned to Lucas and asked, "What the hell are you supposed to be again?"

Lucas looked at Wade, then away as if offended. "Aw, come on," Lucas said. A blue jumpsuit, black work boots, a bowler's cap. He could have almost been anyone. Carey knew, but he wasn't about to spoil the fun, especially if it meant helping his brother. He enjoyed seeing him squirm. "Am I seriously the only one who—okay. I'm Grady Sullivan. You know, the main killer from *Emancipation Day IV*?"

"I'm unfamiliar," Wade said, the contempt oozing from his lips in a thick paste. Carey swayed, the straw still wedged between his lips, lost in the music now. He felt like the prize of the party. So what if the two most important men in his life were having a little tiff? This was a night to remember.

"Well, that Cosmo's place nailed the details. Fucking fantastic, really. If I didn't know better, I'd think they stole it from the set. Amazing they could even pull something like this off. Especially because he changes his look so much throughout the film, and this outfit is from the most intense scene, where he takes an old, dull spoon to this chick's eye and scoops—"

"I'll take your word for it."

"Well, they did a fabulous job on my outfit, too, Wade," Carey said. "You really should have gotten yours—oooh . . . look at that big fuzzy bitch over there dancing with Kat Dyer." He squealed with faux-feminine delight, then pointed to a giant furry blue fox tiptoeing around as if it were lost in a Looney Tunes cartoon. The fox slid and grooved, getting every inch possible out of its costume.

"Lucky bastard, whoever he is," Lucas said. "I'd slice open my left nut and pour in a pint of salted lemon juice just for the chance to hear Kat fart through an ear horn."

"Ooookay," Wade said, trying to whistle his way out of the convo. He looked like he was done with this party, with this whole scene. He probably just wanted to go home and suckle on a couple of ice cold wine coolers or snort some blow in private, watch some *Golden Girls* reruns, have some sloppy sex, and call it a night.

"Aren't you seeing that bimbo Beth Weston now or something?" Carey asked.

"Yeah," Lucas said. "I guess. Barely. So?"

"Well, I guess she gets what she paid for," Wade said.

"Who paid for what, guy?" a female voice behind them asked. Its timber hovered between meekness and confidence. A pale, thin arm hooked through Lucas's arm. With her free hand, she lightly patted Lucas's crotch. "I get my goodies for free, you know."

"Oh, hey Beth," Lucas said, attempting to sound as if both of his heads were happy to see her. Carey went back to sipping his beverage. He sized up his brother's latest fling, a perfect blonde Barbie princess, about as tiny as a young woman could be without being mistaken for a child. Her costume did not help matters much. A baby doll, complete with a pink bow tied in her hair, a giant lollipop, white knee-highs, and four-inch pumps. Sexy by the straight male population's shallow standards and probably had a snatch that clung like a vice, but Carey was sure Beth's brain was pudding. Her inner core was hollow. So, so hollow.

"You about ready to bail?" Beth asked. "This party kinda sucks."

"What . . . not enough coke for your tastes?"

"The blow here is crap. Not even remotely pure. 'sides, I'd rather have benzos anyway. I need to mellow the fuck out. Like, stat."

Carey watched as Kat ended her dance with the blue fox and trotted away. The blue fox shimmied to a table loaded with hors d'oeuvres and a bowl of beer in the center. From a pocket in its side, the fox pulled out a silver flask and poured its thick contents into the bowl.

"Well, hello," Lucas said, guiding Beth's face toward the scene at the punch bowl. "I think I want to stay for a little while."

"Oooh . . . mystery drink. Maybe this night won't be so bad after all."

It seemed like it took a full minute for the flask to empty, but no one else in the room seemed to notice. Or care. Carey figured one high was no less interesting than another at this particular party, and he was perfectly comfortable with having options.

The fox stirred the syrupy liquid with a ladle, mixing the concoction well. Its mask almost appeared to be smiling.

"Well, hell," Lucas said, "far be it from me to pass up an opportunity for a little fun. You coming, little brother—er, sister . . . .whatever."

"Damn straight I am."

"I-*ron*-y," Wade said in a cheeky voice. Lucas and Beth were already at the bowl and ladling up their liquid.

"Whatever," Carey said. "I just want to drink myself to sleep and forget who I am."

"And this is different from any other night how, exactly?"

"Touché." Carey stroked Wade's chin lightly, pecked him on the cheek, then cocked his head in the direction of the punch bowl, which was already becoming more popular among the other partygoers. Apparently they *had* noticed. He skipped over to the table and tried to find an open spot to squeeze his tiny body into.

"Heaven knows, I certainly want to erase this bore of a night," Wade said, following his lover and his lover's brother and his lover's brother's lover to their respective fates.

CHAPTER FIVE

SOMEONE DRESSED AS Joseph Stalin spilled cocaine cut with Ajax or talcum powder or something equally healthy. Its snowflake dust settled in the air, and the remainder landed all over the front of Kat Dyer's dress, but she didn't bother to wipe it off. It blended well enough with the white for her to live with it. Maybe it would still be there later, and she could scrape some off if she was feeling adventurous.

The stereo blared some awful reggaeton performed by a mush-mouthed man of indeterminate racial origin. Kat was not buzzed enough to find this music appealing. Not even close. She hoped to reach that point and beyond before the party ended, to eradicate any evidence of memory from tonight's experiences. It didn't hurt to wish for things that were actually attainable. Alcohol made many things in life feasible.

A few more steps and she accidentally opened the door to the guest bathroom she was sure was Hannah's bedroom but wasn't, walked in on Vampire Hooters Girl and Spongebob Squarepants in the midst of some twisted half-naked make-out session. She caught glimpses of part of a boob, and perhaps a testicle or two hidden within a jungle of pubic hair. Half-snorted coke lined the mosaic countertop like racing stripes. This shit was everywhere. It was practically turning Hannah's house into a winter wonderland. Kat squeaked a "sorry," squeezed herself through another hallway that seemed to get progressively narrower either through design or as a result of human congestion. Its walls were decorated with a cornucopia of autographed celebrity photos. Hannah's father was some big shot producer of some big shit films and really liked to show off who he knew in the "biz."

Kat was on the verge of giving up, but she soon found herself in Hannah's living room, the giant centerpiece of the labyrinthine house.

And there was Hannah. She was a mermaid. Her strawberry hair would have tasted good in a smoothie. She wore seashells on her C-cups. Her shiny fish tail geisha-d her to an enormous cushiony couch that resembled mutant marshmallows. She was pure seaborne sex and she knew it. Young, fit men surrounded her like she was Cleopatra, but Kat had already seen Cleopatra passed out in the laundry room, drenched in a pool of her own vomit.

The men did not notice Kat. Probably too wrapped up talking about the latest Whittier lacrosse team drama. When Hannah saw Kat, she broke character and squealed. She stretched out her arms, begging for Kat to come and give her best girlfriend a ginormous hug, to which Kat complied. A Hannah hug always brought the happies.

Hannah bobbed her head to the beat as she spoke, moved her left hand with a groove like the waves of a mellow ocean. "Kat. Babe. This costume is *so* cool. Feels so grody and, you know . . . real. I never thought I'd see anyone—least of all *you*—attempt Freddy Krueger."

"I don't know who that is. I don't—"

"Don't remember him ever being a crossdresser, though, but maybe I missed that sequel. Can't keep up. Whatevs."

"I don't think that's what *this* is, though." Kat glanced over Hannah's head, through the wall-length window that offered a lush view of Laurel Canyon during the daylight hours, but now only showcased a black, bottomless pit. The girls were just a hop, skip, and a jump away from the site of the Wonderland murders that occurred before either of them was even a worm in the womb. But what happened after tonight would make that event look like an episode of *Mr. Rogers' Neighborhood*. After tonight, everything these girls once knew before would change and rearrange. First kisses would be like foggy dreams from another person's life. Menstruation would seem like a blessing. Cowards would switch roles with the chivalrous. Rigid cocks would go permanently flaccid at the memory. Reality would collide with the chimerical.

"Well, whatever," Hannah said. "Ugly is the new pretty. Sit. *Sit*." She patted the cushion next to her. It retained an imprint of her hand for a few seconds before returning to normal.

"So . . . I just saw Jack," Kat said, struggling to find the balance between talking at a reasonable volume and yelling until she was hoarse. She examined the cushion for any trace of undesirable bodily fluids before immersing her behind into its warm embrace. She sank in and heavily considered never getting up, just letting the couch swallow her whole, an offering to the furniture gods.

"Ooooo, yeah? Was wondering if he was here. Gonna finally get some of that sweet nerd meat tonight?" Hannah clicked her tongue, a habit Kat loathed about her friend, one that Hannah had carried with her since they first met in the 8th grade. It made her sound like a dolphin trying to learn remedial echolocation.

"Um . . . if you say so. I just can't figure him out."

"What's to figure out? The tension's been building for what—five or six years now or whatever? Seems pretty simple to me. He's got an Oscar Meyer and you've got a bun, so pretend it's the Fourth of July and get to cookin' out, right?"

"I don't know. Maybe I—"

A young man with giant fake breasts attached to his chest ran through the living room, screaming like he just won the lottery, perhaps chasing a ghost. Glass shattered in the background. Unseen partiers howled with primal intoxication. Hannah grimaced and struggled to get up, but her fish tail was keeping her immobile for the night. She turned to Jonah, one of her nearby male admirers—the only one whose name Kat remembered because he was also the only one she had seen with Hannah more than once—snapped her fingers, and said, "Would you mind going to check that out? Pretty please with stevia on top? Daddy will have a full-fledged conniption if anyone shits on his garden statues again."

Jonah was a young warrior pulled from ancient Sparta and misplaced in the modern world. Arctic blue eyes. An immaculately trimmed chinstrap beard. Thick, wavy hair—shiny and dark like molasses. Pectorals flexing of their own volition, nipples like polished red pebbles. Calves like thick steel cables and biceps that put those to shame. A living statue of Atlas without that pesky world weighing him down. The only things that shattered the illusion were his bloodshot eyes, his dilated pupils.

Kat absently wiped at her mouth, expecting there to be drool in need of cleaning. She took a sip of her lukewarm beer and tried to pretend she liked it. A nice slice of beefcake could make her sloppy and help her forget all about the boy she really wanted, as temporary as that slip might be.

Without a word, Jonah the boy toy scampered off to do Hannah's bidding.

"Boys," Hannah said, her eyes rolling. "What else are they good for?"

Kat shrugged. "Someone's getting laid, I guess."

"Well, one of us has to, right?" Hannah pursed her lips and wiggled her eyebrows. This always made Kat laugh and Hannah knew it. Tonight was no exception. Kat welcomed the pleasant release. She responded by affecting an oh-so-sophisticated expression and waving her index and middle fingers in front of her lips as if they held an invisible cigarette.

"I'm thinking of maybe joining a convent. One-night stands are so passé. Piety is in, my gorgeous ginger friend."

"Agreed! Remember last Halloween, when I was dressed as a nun? At Beth Weston's warehouse party? I ran into Mason Douglas there and he was dressed like the Pope or something and we went to the abandoned church next door and—"

"I really don't want to know what sort of sick stuff went on. Jack and I took off early for a reason and—"

"But it was *soooo* fun. I mean, come *on*. What could be better than blasphemous intercourse?"

"I wouldn't know."

"Oh, you're no fun, Kat."

"Just keep that one in the vault, yeah?"

"Ppppp. Fine." Hannah motioned to a marble cheese plate sitting on the table in front of her. Kat picked it up and passed it to her immobile mermaid friend. Four perfectly aligned tally marks of snow. Hannah grabbed a rolled-up hundred-dollar bill from the plate, shoved it in her nose, and snorted a line. She offered the plate to Kat, and Kat happily accepted the gift. She needed a pick-me-up, post-haste. Forget about the crap that was stuck to her dress. Hannah's stash was undoubtedly purer.

Jonah returned, practically saluting his master Hannah, then continued his previous conversation with the young man next to him, who was dressed as a hot dog. Subtlety was overrated.

"Crisis averted," Hannah said. "No kissing Daddy's ass this time. Not that he knows this is even going on."

"Mm-hmm. Sure he doesn't. Hey, the night's still young, too. All kinds of bad things could happen."

"Don't jinx my party, girl. I'll have to—"

"Sweetie, I'm sorry. I'm going to have to pick up this convo later." Kat placed her hand on Hannah's tail where she assumed her thigh would be and squeezed lightly. "I'm going to try and find Jack again, see what the hell's wrong with him."

"Hell yeah, hot stuff. Get him to rip that weird jerky off your body with his teeth."

"Doubt it, but thanks for the support. You're a crazy bitch and I love you lots." Kat blew Hannah a kiss and Hannah caught it and pretended to tie it into her hair.

All seemed to be well in the House of Hannah, and so Kat scurried away to track down Jack, leaving her best friend and her beau-for-the-night in a position where they might soon liquor each other up and stumble to Hannah's parents' room, somehow figure out how to copulate in spite of Hannah's fish tail, hit a grand slam in the Impregnation World Series, and quietly get married at the courthouse a year later "for the sake of the baby." Or not.

Kat weaved through the house, her sights set on anything remotely blue. She almost tripped over a passed-out partygoer whose body was painted like a Smurf. Soon she located Jack the furry fox, his back to her, apparently still dancing by himself. This was so unlike him. What the hell was he on, and where could she get some?

The rest of the party had given him a wide berth to do his thing. Jack sounded like he was grunting—no—giggling. He turned around, paused when his fox head presumably noticed Kat, then wiggled his finger toward his body, beckoning her to come closer. Kat threw her hands up in frustration, took a step toward him, and he skittered out of the room.

Though Kat was not in the mood for games, she figured Jack wanted her to follow him for some important reason, so she did. Maybe he thought he was getting some sort of secret kiss or something along those lines. Wasn't happening. Not tonight, as bad as she wanted it. Jack always was a little too confident for his own good.

Or maybe not. Maybe Kat would be generous enough or maybe she was jacked enough to dish out a quick lip dip. It would be about time. Jack would have to put on his sweet voice before she gave it any serious consideration. Then again, he pretty much always had his sweet voice on. That was part of the problem. She never knew if he was sweet on her or just sweet in general. She hoped it was both.

She followed Jack outside, past the pool and some swimmers who had chosen to forego their costumes for the evening in exchange for partial or complete nudity, into a cabana that appeared to be set up as some sort of guest room. Despite spending more time at Hannah's house than she could measure, Kat had no recollection of ever seeing this structure before. With a lot the size of the Harper estate, this wasn't much of a surprise. They could build to their heart's content and never run out of square footage.

The walls of the cabana were adorned with pretentiously priced abstract art that had no business being this close to a swimming pool, and the ceiling was made of glass, revealing twinkles from the few stars that had decided to do their jobs tonight.

Jack stopped just inches from Kat. She could feel the heat of his breath seeping through the mask, filling up this enclosed space. She felt dizzy and nauseated. He grabbed her arm, gripped it tight, and pulled her close. He clumsily groped at her body, her breasts, her ass. She tried to beat him away, but she wasn't strong enough, wasn't large enough. Height didn't help much if muscle wasn't accompanying it.

Her heart was doing calisthenics. She couldn't figure out what had gotten into Jack, aside from maybe way too much alcohol or likely something stronger. He had always been her safe haven in human form, never showed even a remote sign of aggression toward her. Now she was trying to reconcile the fact that her image of him might be ruined, perhaps irrevocably.

She squirmed and struggled some more until he finally let go.

"What the fuck, Jack? What the hell is wrong with you, asshole?" She punched him as hard as her tiny fist would allow, which was admittedly pretty hard, solid enough to make him jerk back. It hurt her hand, and she resisted the urge to show it. She couldn't appear weak. Not now.

A hollow laugh came from within the mask. As he removed it a waterfall of sweat poured out.

Kat heaved and whipped her hand toward her mouth. She turned and ran from the cabana, racing toward the pool, barely making it there before a stream of vomit erupted from her mouth. The candy corn colors dissolved and spread throughout the chlorinated water. The few swimming partygoers screamed words of disgust and got out of the pool. Kat crouched and waited for the next hurl. A pair of black boots stomped next to her, then legs clad in torn jeans crouched next to her. A gentle hand caressed the back of her neck and pulled her hair away from her face to prevent it from being further soaked in puke.

"Hey, Kitty Kat," the voice attached to the boots and jeans and gentle hand said. Only one person had ever been allowed to call her by that silly nickname, but he was the one person this could not possibly have been. Except it was. "Hannah said you were probably out here. Geez, you're such a lightweight." She struggled and pushed herself into a kneeling position, then turned to see a familiar face smirking behind a pair of thick glasses, a Wolf Man mask lying on the ground in front of him. It took Kat longer than it should have to realize who this was. She was confused mostly because the laws of physics did not allow for this sort of discrepancy.

"J-Jack?"

"It's okay. I'm here. You're safe. Everything's going to be alright."

CHAPTER SIX

"**R**EALLY? THAT'S THE best you could come up with, dude? I mean . . . *really*?"

"Hey, fuck you, Jack. It's not like the Wolf Man thing is some huge revelation. Oooh, baby. You're so original. Don't hold your breath, 'cause you're not winning any high-end costume contests tonight." Edgar Cotton stood in the doorway to his bedroom. He wore a child-sized plastic pug mask that only covered his face and somewhat muffled his gravelly voice, as well as a t-shirt fittingly exclaiming "PUG LIFE."

"Simple, yet effective, bud." Jack noticed Edgar was not wearing anything below the waist save for a pair of fuzzy slippers and dirty grey boxer briefs that might have recently served as a smorgasbord for moths. Edgar scratched his ass and snorted mucous up into his nasal cavity without missing a beat.

"Yeah, whatever. Hey, there wasn't much left at that stupid costume place anyway. I mean—the only other semi-suitable choice was like some Godzilla-looking wannabe motherfucker."

"Too expensive, I guess?" Jack removed his black-rimmed glasses and put his mask on, then put the glasses back on. It didn't suit the costume well, but a man had to be able to see.

"Well, yeah. I probably dodged a bullet with that one. Would have been sweating like a bastard all night. Plus, I've already got a monster in my pants. Honk, honk." Edgar cupped his crotch, smirked with no reaction from Jack, and pulled on a pair of faded blue jeans. He'd never been one to fully commit to a costume. Or to a job. Or much of anything, really.

"True. Except for that last part. You ready yet?"

"Almost." Edgar popped a blue butterfly pill into his mouth and swallowed it dry. He offered one to Jack.

Jack shook his head. "Not tonight. Well, maybe later. We'll see how bored I get. Probably I'll get pretty bored. God, I fucking hate parties."

"I know. You're just such a fun guy. I love you so much, dude."

"Cram it."

Edgar squirted some cologne underneath his arms. Jack thought it smelled like it might be at least 10 percent coyote urine.

"There," Edgar said. "Edgar's ready to party hardy now. Let's motor."

———————— ◆ ————————

As the young men passed through the double doorway leading into Hannah Harper's house and entered the foyer, Edgar let loose an unfathomably loud howl, followed by a "Ladies, come and get it!" Despite his best efforts, the booming music made it impossible for anyone outside of their immediate proximity to hear, which amounted to a fat girl dressed as Olive Oil and two male professional wrestlers Jack did not recognize.

"You know," Jack said, yelling even though he was inches away from Edgar's ear, "my folks had a pug when I was a kid. They aren't exactly known for their bellowing. It's more of a grunty wheeze." He did his best attempt at an imitation but ended up sounding like someone with emphysema.

"And that's what the right lady will receive when she gives a dog a chance."

Jack rolled his eyes, forgetting he was wearing a mask. "You're a real peach, man."

"Isn't that why you adopted me and gave me a forever home?"

"They're also the Praeder-Willies of the dog world."

"Say what? Speak English."

"Never mind. Come on. Let's go find Kat."

"Shit. Someone's a little desperate, yeah?"

Jack socked Edgar in the shoulder, perhaps a little too hard because it actually stunned him and shut him up for a few seconds.

They wound through the mazelike living quarters. Edgar was briefly distracted by a fine specimen of college-aged womanhood in a Slave Leia costume, then was briefly guided back into reality when Leia was joined by a rather large brute whose body was practically bursting through his army fatigues. They passed by a bowl filled with sticky candy corn. Edgar took a small handful, lifted his mask, and shoveled the candy into his mouth. Jack looked at the bowl and grimaced.

It felt like hours before they were able to find a reliable source of alcohol. A punch bowl that was likely overflowing with liquor when the party started, but now barely had enough liquid to fill the remaining red cups. They grabbed their drinks while they had the chance. Jack hoped there was more elsewhere. There had to at least be a keg outside. Hannah wouldn't let her friends down.

Edgar lifted his mask, chugged a full cup, scooped another serving, and they moved on. They squeezed through a tight hallway and Jack tried to pretend he didn't see Edgar mashing against multiple girls and "apologizing" for the indiscretion. They were soon spit out into a large room where they found Hannah, and it was immediately clear to Jack who her favorite Disney character was. Her fish tail was draped across the lap of a well-chiseled young man dressed as some sort of gladiator. Jack locked eyes with Hannah and nodded his head upward. She squinted, likely trying to discern who he was. He removed his mask, and she then shot him a warm grin and beckoned to him with a large gesture, both of her hands flapping toward her like she was trying to fan herself.

Jack headed toward Hannah and her couch, which could have doubled as a heavenly cloud. Edgar clamped his shoulder and said, "Hey, I'll catch up with you later. I think I just saw Beth."

"Your funeral."

Edgar sipped his drink, winked, and disappeared into the crowd. Jack made his way to the couch and plopped down without an official invite to sit. Hannah planted a wet kiss on his cheek. "Hiya, dork," she said.

"What's up? Seen Kat yet tonight?"

"What am I—chopped tuna?" Hannah giggled at her own funny.

"No, no . . . I just—"

"I'm kidding, dummy. You just missed her. She went to go find you again, actually. Said you were acting weird or something. I dunno."

"Huh?"

"Huh what?"

"Find me 'again'?"

Hannah looked baffled for a moment, then abandoned the plot thread. "Oh, hey, have you met Jonah before?" She motioned to the gladiator who had thus far not acknowledged Jack's presence, but now responded to his own name. His eyes indicated he was high on something that was going to keep him docile for the next few hours. Hannah introduced them. Jack offered his hand for a traditional shake, but Jonah returned with a fist. Jack paused briefly and bumped it with his own fist. He supposed this made them bros now. Men in good standing with one another did not need to exchange petty pleasantries.

"Jonah, sweetheart, can you rub my toe again?" Hannah asked. "I can't reach."

Jonah massaged Hannah's toe-buried-beneath-a-tail and turned back to his conversation with a guy in a hot dog outfit.

"So, yeah," Hannah continued, "is this guy a hunk or what? Oh, what am I telling you for? Like you even care. I'm such a—"

"Wait. Hannah. Hold on. What's this about Kat saying I was acting weird? I saw her this afternoon and everything seemed cool. I—"

"No, sweetie. She meant from like a few minutes ago. Like from here. You know, you put on a good sober face, but you're obviously zonked out of your mind."

"Hannah, I don't . . . me and Edgar, we just got here. I haven't even seen her yet. You're the only person I've even talked to beyond a 'hello' or whatever."

"Hmm . . . well that's kinda weird."

"Or maybe I have. I'm not even sure what her costume is. She wouldn't let me see it earlier. Shit, what if I didn't recognize her and blew her off. She's gonna be so—"

"Trust me . . . you'd know if you saw her." Hannah looked down at her cuticle and dug at it with a nail from her opposite hand.

"Are you sure she said she—"

"I mean—she wasn't, like, high or anything. She might be a little fucked up now, though. Whatever, though. I think she went thataway." Hannah lunged her head in the general direction of the backyard, toward the swimming pool.

"Okay, thanks. I'll bring her back and we'll all hang or something."

"Yeah, totally. And if you don't, no biggie, just don't forget to come say bye before you leave at least."

"Of course."

"Go get her, tiger." Hannah clicked her tongue and Jack set off to find Kat and figure out what the hell Hannah was talking about. Even if he had accidentally blown Kat off, she'd understand. A simple mistake warranted a simple apology, and they would move on with the night and the rest of their lives. Easiest resolution in the world.

Before Jack reached the sliding glass door that led outside, he saw a familiar face waiting in line for the restroom. Beth Weston. Her golden hair was twisted into curls held together with pink bows. No toddler would have been caught dead in her risqué outfit. She held a gigantic swirling lollipop. She did not see Jack approaching.

"Hey," he said, causing Beth to jerk and jump just a bit. "Edgar find you yet?"

"Oh. Hi." Beth rolled her eyes. Her voice was pure valley. "Unfortunately, yeah. I told him to fuck off."

"You know, I realize I'm biased and all, but that little jerk really does love you. He'd never admit it, but he talks about you all the goddamn time. And he'll kick my ass if he ever finds out I breathed a word of this to you."

"If he, like, thinks he even has a sliver of a chance of getting back together, his groveling is going to need to be *epic*. Doesn't matter anyway. I'm dating Lucas now."

"Uh-huh. You mean fucking Lucas while he bides his time until the next clueless chick comes along."

"Same difference. Oh, hey, can you hold this for me while I go pee?" She extended her absurd lollipop to Jack, but he backed off, his palms flat in the air.

"Sorry. On my way to find Kat."

"Ugh. Fine."

Jack took a few steps backward and offered Beth a friendly wave goodbye, the friendly part fabricated. He turned around and plowed right into someone wearing a blue fox costume. The fox grunted and shoved Jack out of the way before he had the chance to apologize, then stomped away, only pausing to grab Beth's almost bare ass. Beth squealed and jumped, called the blue fox an asshole, and for a moment she looked like she was considering throwing her lollipop at him. However, she did not budge, likely because she was next in line for the restroom. Wasn't worth the risk. She and Jack exchanged shocked expressions. Jack shrugged and dashed off. He passed through the doorway to the backyard and expected fresh air to hit him, but there were puffs of both marijuana and cigarette smoke in almost every direction.

After carefully considering a couple of similarly small-framed girls, he saw Kat kneeling next to the pool. A layer of vomit floated near the edge. People were scattering and complaining. He fought against the traffic coming his way and finally made it to Kat's side. He crouched next to her, dropped his Wolf Man mask, and rubbed the back of her neck with one hand, pulling the hair away from her face to give her room to breathe.

"Hey, Kitty Kat," he said. "Hannah said you were probably out here. Geez, you're such a lightweight." He almost laughed but stifled it at the last second.

Kat turned in his direction and pushed herself up into a kneeling position.

"J-Jack?"

"It's okay. I'm here. You're safe. Everything's going to be alright."

"Don't touch me!" Kat shoved his hand away and sat on the concrete.

"Whoah . . . hey, I'm not gonna hurt you Kat. It's just me. What the hell is wrong?"

"I . . . I don't understand," Kat said. "How'd you . . . change so quick? You seem like you . . . but you didn't . . . blue . . . fox." Jack wiped excess gunk from her lips with the arm of his torn-to-shreds flannel shirt. Even her puke didn't faze him. Kat smiled at him, trying and failing to be an object of desire. So pathetically beautiful in her moment of need.

"I don't know what you mean, you weirdo. I've been trying to track you down ever since I got here. This fucking house is like a maze. I swear, no matter how many times I've been here I still get—"

"But . . . I . . . you were just in . . . " Kat made an attempt to gesture toward the cabana. She looked down at his mask, then back at his face. "Blue. Fox . . . right?"

"Wait—you thought that blue fox creep was me? Oh, thanks a lot!"

"No. Yes. Well . . . I dunno. I think...I . . . drunk . . . sick. Something."

"You know, I'd like to think I'd make better decisions than that guy." Jack's face warped in some twisted form of anger. "He didn't try to do anything to you, did he? Like, hurt you?"

"No. Almost. Well, yeah, but . . . I guess he could have, but . . . " Kat started sobbing.

"God, what a dickfuck. Only an asshole would try to fuck with my Kitty Kat." Jack helped Kat stand, pulled her into a warm embrace, and she ceased sobbing. He could feel her breathing slowly. She was focused. Calmed. Her costume chafed him, but he tried to ignore it. She opened her eyes, looked at him, and her face scrunched up in fearful pain.

"What's wrong?"

Kat attempted to point toward his cheek. "Who . . . kissed?"

Jack raised his eyebrows and wondered what the hell she was talking about, then remembered. He laughed.

"Hannah. Just Hannah."

"Oh. Cool."

"But Kat? Since we're on the topic of confusing costumes . . . " Jack's nose made an exaggerated sniffing motion.

"Hmm?"

"How many lives were lost to provide that outfit for you? Yeesh." He stood up, extended his hand to help Kat to her feet. "What the hell are you supposed to be anyway?"

CHAPTER SEVEN

I T WAS THE morning after Halloween, smack dab in the center of what some cultures refer to as *Día de los Muertos*, but there were no sugar skulls or marigold petals or melted candles decorating Hannah Harper's house. Only dry, stale vomit and contorted, hungover sleeping bodies and uneaten, crumbled snack remnants. The sun had just barely crept out its grave and was peeking over the horizon, perhaps hoping at least a few people in the house would curse it when they awakened. It is a little-known fact that the sun revels in such an experience, especially when its victims' heads are already pounding like the inside of a bass drum.

Ken Meyer, always an early riser, was perhaps the first to notice the invading light, though it was filtered through a brownish haze, like someone had spread a light layer of paint over his eyes. Whatever those unlabeled pills were that Jonah had shared with him last night, they were potent enough to force him to crash out on Hannah's living room floor.

The room looked bigger than it should have, likely an optical illusion resulting from the final moments of the high. The shuffling and snoring sounds around him were muffled, yet also absurdly loud. He couldn't wrap his mind around that strange contradiction. He took a deep breath, but felt no clean oxygen enter his lungs. The air was stuffy. He struggled and squirmed and willed his body to get up, but he couldn't move. It was as if someone had played a party prank on him while passed out, wrapped his body in plastic wrap or glued his arms to his sides. But scarier than that, two steps away from being buried alive. At least he felt cushioned, his whole back and both sides hugged by something soft and slightly moist. A minor consolation.

Jonah . . . .whathahellhappename? Ken said. The sound did not exit his mouth, only reverberated in his mind. Echoed and bounced and quivered. A thought that could never be heard. *Wheredafuggareyou?*

As if his cry for help were being answered, Jonah's face suddenly hovered over his own, dulled by the brownish canopy Ken still couldn't explain.

There was only one problem, but it was a fairly significant one: Jonah's face was considerably larger than it should have been, as was the rest of his body. From Ken's perspective, Jonah appeared to have just come down the beanstalk.

Ken screamed, blamed it on the pills again, but Jonah did not even flinch. He only stared. It was no poker face. It was something much, much worse. A look of desperate hunger. Hangover hunger.

"Oh shit," Jonah said. "Who left this here?" The voice exploded, causing a hefty ringing in Ken's eardrums. Ken screamed again and the reverberations were nightmarish. The sensation was so disorienting that Ken barely noticed when Jonah picked him up and cradled him in his hand. That was the moment he knew he was dreaming, had to be. And what a mindfuck of a dream it was. He wanted the hell out of it. He willed himself to wake up. No dice.

"Hey, Ken . . . get over here, man," Jonah said, his voice booming. He looked around, confused. "Nothing like a free hot dog to cure the hangover blues. Christ, where the hell is he?" It was then that Ken had his horrifying epiphany.

His costume. Last night. A hot dog. That was what he chose last minute at that place on Ventura Boulevard everyone was going to. Time was running out and he had to have *something* to wear for Hannah's party. He wasn't going to be the one jerk who showed up sans costume. It was cheap, convenient, almost funny if not terribly original. Ken laughed and wailed and shrieked and spit because he knew now that this really had to be just some absurd Kafka-esque dream caused by too many cocktails and cupcakes and failed sexual advances, one that felt more real than it should have, one filled with noticeable sounds and sights and smells.

But it wasn't. Scents and sounds and utter awareness couldn't exist in the world of dreams. Not in the way these sensations do in the actual world. Those were the rules. Senses existed only as distortions, or perhaps the senses in dreams were real, and what was heard and smelled in the wakened world was a falsehood. Ken couldn't believe he was being philosophical at a moment like this.

The smell. It was lingering before, but now—with his senses heightened—the stench was more evident. A mix of asshole meat and pungent tomato.

Jonah's enormous face looked down upon him, and for one second Ken thought there was recognition in his eyes. But he was so very wrong. Did a man ever recognize the face in his meal? Jonah lightly brushed the top of Ken's body, and it felt like a bicycle running over him. Then Jonah mumbled, "No bugs. Looks all right to me," but the mumble turned into a rumble. Ken could see a pimple in the corner of Jonah's nose, the only blemish he had ever seen on his friend, the kind of milky white intruder that could only appear as a result of an extremely rough night. A light film of perspiration transformed into a tiny snowcapped mountain. But Ken could see it up close, more than anyone would ever hope to witness a zit. His eyes were like magnifying glasses. He felt dizzy. He wanted to scream again.

When Jonah took the first bite, Ken didn't really have a choice.

Ken's first scream after the bite tore his larynx, made his earlier screams seem like mere whispers. There is regular pain and then there is pain that can only be felt by those who are being eaten alive. It's a unique sensation. However, victims of sharks and gators at least have a precedent that has been set. Something to expect. No man has ever been eaten by his best friend in the form of an unhealthy morning snack, something that might cost two for a dollar on the right day at the right fast food joint.

Ken should have felt something snap, a femur or tibia or fibula, but instead experienced a sinewy tearing sensation where his legs had once been. Though the sounds of his own hoarse screams only echoed within his own head, Ken couldn't stop because at least it reminded him he was still alive, if only for a few moments longer.

He felt something slimy near his midsection and, in a moment of clarity, realized he was probably shitting himself.

Jonah made a slightly disgusted face, then took another bite, wasting no time trying to gulp his snack down. He had always been a fast eater, and Ken remembered in a moment of honest and ironic humor that Jonah had placed second in a hot dog eating contest freshman year at Whittier. This morning he was only slowed down by his hangover. Jonah released a belch and Ken caught a whiff of burning hot wind laced with stale beer. Ken began to hyperventilate. He was fading fast.

Another bite, this one clumsier, like Jonah had to stop to catch a drop of ketchup with his tongue. Unbearable slurping sounds. Ken's midsection exploded and he passed out in shock, mercifully did not feel the final few bites that would lead him on the path down the gastrointestinal tract, eventually passing through his best friend's anus and finding his final resting place in some indeterminate sewer among the filthy damp rats, albino cockroaches, and colonies of pulsating worms.

———————◆———————

Jonah was more than halfway through his hot dog before he realized something wasn't right. The taste was off. He wondered if a hot dog could go bad overnight, if in fact it had been cooked last night. He sure as hell hoped it wouldn't have been made any earlier than that. As famished as he was, now he wasn't sure if he wanted to keep eating it. Maybe if he stopped now he could avoid getting sick. Or at least get less sick.

He looked at the wiener on a bun, contemplating taking another bite. Something oozed from its center. For a split second he thought it might be one of those dogs filled with pasteurized cheese, but then realized that was something poor people bought with food stamps, not the kind of cuisine you'd find in the Harper household.

He examined the hot dog more closely. The ooze was definitely not cheese. It was brown, dark green maybe. His stomach complained. He licked his teeth. He looked closer. His heart twitched. He saw something that couldn't be unseen, something that couldn't have been real.

A familiar face.

Jonah dropped the hot dog and ran toward the restroom, just as Hannah screamed his name.

CHAPTER EIGHT

CAREY DIDN'T EXPECT to be beautiful when he woke up the day after Halloween. He had never looked even halfway presentable when hung over, and this particular holiday tended to bring out the extreme lush in him. It's not so much that he was a messy drunk. But, truth be told, there were times when he'd woken up with jockey shorts that weren't his (or Wade's) attached to his head like a cornette, times when he'd willingly performed almost perfect karaoke to a Rick Astley song, times when he might or might not have eaten an entire rhubarb pie in one sitting. But now he stood in front of the mirror, his makeup from the previous night smeared into raccoon formation, his hair the victim of severe bedhead.

His hair.

His hair was the first problem that sobered him up pretty damned quickly. This wasn't his hair at all. Carey kept it buzzed close to the scalp, mostly as a result of premature thinning, but also because Wade seemed to have a thing for rubbing his hands all over that peach fuzz head, which was admittedly sort of a turn on. Thus, the wig last night for Hannah's party. It was necessary for full-blown faux-bombshell status. He certainly wouldn't have opted for a Sinead O'Connor look. Far too butch.

Now it felt like the wig wouldn't budge, like some asshole had glued it to his head after he passed out sometime in the wee hours. Of course, since he had slept over at Wade's house that asshole would have to be his own boyfriend. Pranking wasn't Wade's style, though. His sense of humor was typically limited to dirty limericks and misquoted dialogue from *Fawlty Towers*. Yet, even though it was a 100% authentic human hair wig according to the bushy-browed clerk who sold it to him, it now felt somehow silkier and more natural than it should, especially after sleeping in it.

Carey's eyes traveled south along the mirror. He realized he was still wearing the black party dress. Had he really been so wasted that he hadn't even bothered to undress?

It was at this moment he discovered his problems were far, far worse than the dark mop seemingly glued to his head.

Though he'd managed to make last night's false cleavage look convincing with a combination of custom-made breast forms and meticulous makeup, it definitely wouldn't have fooled a sober man. Not that there had been one at the party to test that theory on. However, now the breasts were proper milk mountains, ready to burst through the dress if he shifted the wrong way. The three-dimensional crevice of cleavage was no optical illusion, and Carey wedged his fingers between the breasts to confirm this. The meat on each side of his sternum was round and soft, the space between tight enough to hold a pencil upright. He had heard of urban legends where people awoke in a bathtub full of ice, drugged up and missing a kidney. Could a boob job be performed under similar circumstances? And if it could, where was the swelling, the incision? Why was he not in throbbing pain? None of this made any sense.

Carey's instincts kicked in. Terror streaked his face in a clownish silent scream. He slowly moved his hands down his tight, yet now slightly curvy midsection, a motion that might have been sensual under different circumstances. A real Marilyn Monroe moment. He inched toward his crotch. Last night, he had worn a pair of laced underwear to add authenticity to his costume. It was still clinging tight to his pelvis. God had not graced him with a terribly majestic prick—average at best, and for a split-second Carey believed he just hadn't found the little guy yet, that maybe Carey Jr. had decided to tuck himself in for a power nap.

Again, he was wrong.

What had once been a modest bulge beneath the slippery satin was now smooth and flat. Carey gulped. He could feel the slight shape of lips, lips he had only known from Sex Ed videos and had always found completely uninteresting. Why bother with a vagina when a perfectly good cock had more versatility, more potential for penetration?

His scream stopped being silent. It grew in volume rapidly, as if controlled by remote. The scream bounced back and forth across the bedroom walls. It sounded like an audition for a slasher movie, multiplied by eleven.

A pillow whacked him in the back.

"Oh. My. God. What the hell, Carey? Please keep it shut. At least go in the living room or something. It feels like a Sumo wrestler is stomping on my head. What in God's name did I take last night?" Wade shifted in the bed, his naked, hairy, perfect body barely covered by the mauve silk sheets. He rubbed his eyes and stared at Carey in disbelief. "Why are you still wearing that frock anyway? You realize there's a reason we didn't fuck last night, right? Me cocky no likey Carey as girly. I don't know why you even bo—"

"Wade! My fucking dick!"

"Exactly. It's your dick I want, not—"

"It's gone! My fucking dick is gone!" Quivering, Carey turned to face Wade.

Wade snorted in that distinct way Carey loathed, the sound that could mean either lines of coke had just disappeared or laughter was on the horizon. "I hate to sound like your mother, but you really shouldn't joke about things like that."

"I'm not kidding. Oh, fuck! Please, Wade. Oh my God I'm really freaked the fuck out!"

"Please. What the hell are you on? Did Lucas score you a blotter last night or something? I swear . . . if he gave you bad acid again, I'll kick his ass so hard he'll wake up dead." Wade leaned over to the nightstand and grabbed his glass of emergency water, took a sip.

"Wade, will you just shut the hell up for a goddamned minute and let me talk? This is a fucking emergency!"

"What's with your voice? Slip too much honey in your morning tea?"

"Please! Just listen to me!"

Carey was on the verge of tears. He was certain this was no dream. He could smell a cloud of morning breath floating throughout the room, could hear the familiar rumble of cars passing along the street, could feel the redistributed weight of his new body—lighter in some places and heavier in others, but completely tangible. He lifted up the dress and pulled down the underwear to show Wade. The proof was in the pussy.

Wade's face went pale.

He dropped his glass of water. The wet shards slid across the wood floor.

———————◆———————

"Holy shit. What the fuck, Carey? This isn't funny. Now I know someone slipped something in my drink last night. Jesus Christ. This is too much!"

"This isn't a joke! Help me! Fucking help me! I don't know what's going on!" Carey was hysterical. Huddled in a ball on the floor, inches from the broken glass, his body vibrating like he was lost in the Arctic with no hope of rescue.

Wade took a deep breath and rubbed his eyes again, turning the crust into butter. He scooted to the edge of the bed, his penis still protected by the sheets. Carey now knelt in front of him, biting his lip, quieting down a bit. Reality, or what was currently passing as reality, sunk in. Wade gestured for Carey to stand again and Carey refused. Wade persisted. Carey reluctantly obeyed.

He reached toward Carey's dress and lifted it up again, the brand new vagina now somewhat exposed. Carey pulled back, and Wade put his hands out to let Carey know he would not hurt him. He never had, so why would he start now?

Wade placed his face mere inches from Carey's waist and examined the fresh genitalia. When Carey had pulled down the panties the first time, Wade was certain he was being fooled by something purchased from the porno shop as a joke. However, upon closer inspection, he realized this was not the case.

Carey's pubes were respectably trimmed, as always, but hiding within the fuzz was something from an alien galaxy. Wade remembered his sister Ellen referring to her vagina as her "special flower" when they were very young. He had begged her to see it. He had to know the truth behind why boys and girls were different. Mom and Dad certainly weren't spilling the beans. Even then, before he understood the power a woman could have over some men, long before he knew which sex he preferred, he couldn't figure out what the big deal was. It was just a small fold, a hole leading to nowhere special. A lamprey eel waiting to prey on the weak flesh of an unsuspecting fish. Big deal.

Now, looking at Carey's hole, Wade wasn't sure whether he wanted to laugh, retch, or both. It was a deliberate piece of fleshy art, but art is subjective and Wade didn't have a particular affinity for this piece. It was much larger than his sister's was back then, but likely the same size as it now was, a thought that made Wade pause in bizarre disgust. He took a deep breath to allow the nausea to subside.

Wade turned away and focused on a framed photograph on the wall. He and Carey, on vacation in San Francisco last year, slumming it in the Castro where Wade swore he would never go again despite secretly having the time of his life. Wade had grown out an ill-advised chinstrap for about a month that was now immortalized in a picture he could never burn. And even if he could, the memory of that extended weekend would remain tattooed in his brain.

He tried to steady his breathing and turned back to face Carey. He placed his hand lightly on Carey's shoulder.

It barely looked like his wonderful boyfriend anymore, the young man he had known in the biblical sense since before either of them was legally able to drive. Carey's eyes were always the prettiest things about him, though, and those were still there, albeit tarted up with long, dark eyelashes and smeared, smoky makeup. Wade never realized until now that those eyes should have been placed in a woman's skull all along. And he felt ill for thinking this.

No, Wade thought. *No they shouldn't have. This is a whole new level of completely fucked. This is the moment when I'm supposed to wake up and have a good laugh.*

"Yeah," Wade said after many minutes of silent observation. "Oh yeah, this is really, really bad. What the . . . Christ, what the hell happened last night?"

Carey shut his mouth for possibly the first time since his infant lips first uttered the word "Mama" and started crying. Wade believed Carey had never truly cried in his life. Not before this morning. He hadn't shed a tear even when their good friend Chaz was beaten to death in a back alley off Santa Monica, not when *Ab Fab* was cancelled, and certainly not even when Wade had first professed his undying love. That would have been just too much to ask. Tears had never been a featured dish on Carey's emotional menu, and Wade was always perfectly fine with this. He was the same way. The last thing he needed was some whining queen wetting up his shoulder every five minutes.

But now Carey wailed and rained and moaned. Wade stood up, his flaccid eight inches pasted to the side of his leg by a combination of sweat and a coarse black jungle of hair. He hugged Carey and felt the fat of his lover's breasts against his chest. The hug was loose, uncomfortable. He patted Carey's back as if he was burping a baby. Everything about it felt wrong, a mockery of comfort.

"I'm sorry," Wade said. "You have to go."

Carey's powerful cries dissolved into smaller sobs. "What?"

"Please, Carey. I just can't right now. I need time to think."

"What the fuck are you talking about? It's me, Wade. I need your help, for fuck's sake. Why would you—"

"Is it? Is it you? Is this real? No, something's not right. This is some sick joke. A very vivid, very bad dream. Please leave." Wade pointed to the door. "We can talk about this later. I don't feel well. I can't . . . I can't look at you . . . not like this."

"You son of a bitch." Carey slapped him with all the fury of a man-turned-woman scorned. It stung so hard it made his cheek numb. But this was only the beginning. Carey turned his palm into a fist and started beating on Wade's chest, then his other hand joined in, connecting hard with the side of Wade's arm. The sharp pain invalidated his hopes that this was all a drug-induced dream. There would be bruises to mend later, some unseen, some that might never heal. Wade took it. He had to. He deserved it and he knew it. "How fucking dare you? After all this time?"

Carey stopped hitting him, but Wade still held his hands up in defense. "It's not permanent. I just need time, just need to figure out what—"

"Don't give me any 'it's not you, it's me' bullshit. Jesus! You proposed to me in a fucking *straight bar* and now I look like a woman and you can't even help me through . . . through *this*? Oh my God, Wade! You fucking scum-sucking disloyal faggot!"

Wade couldn't believe Carey had uttered that slur, and when

he looked in Carey's eyes he knew his lover had instantly regretted it.

"Just go. I'll call you when I'm ready."

Carey stormed out, but not before he found something to break. A glass snow globe prominently featuring Seattle's Space Needle. It shattered across the wood, mixed with the glass and water from Wade's drink.

The glittery snow was all that was left.

CHAPTER NINE

LUCAS LANE HAD been subject to dark thoughts for quite some time, perhaps most of his natural born life. However, this morning he had an epiphany.

It's possible he had never really been what was traditionally considered "good."

Perhaps the first two decades of his life could be thought of as a pupal stage that had been dragged out for far too long. A lie his parents had somehow swindled him into believing so he would behave. *Be a good lil' boy, Lucas, and wonderful things will come your way. Use your privilege to get ahead, wait for the right moment, and take what is rightfully owed to you.* There were far worse lies perpetuated by parents.

He went to church, swallowed the shit that was fed to him, and truly believed that if he behaved like the good Christian his parents shaped him to be, the world would be his for the taking. He was naïve, as young children often are.

Was good just God with an extra vowel? That's what Lucas had been trying to figure out ever since he woke up this morning. Couldn't wrap his mind around it. It was the world's crappiest riddle, and he figured the answer depended on who was defining the word. All evil came from a human source, and at least eighty percent of that evil wasn't pure. It was just co-opted by misguided fools. Human sheep who either had no idea they were doing the wrong thing because their IQ was equal to that of mildew, or those who sincerely thought they were spreading the goody two-shoes gospel.

Lucas was of the opinion that all villains worth their salt truly believed they were doing the right thing. He felt the concept of good was subjective. A concept he'd argued for in Philosophy class his freshman year. He'd brought up Charlie Manson, claiming the cult leader truly believed planning for and even triggering Helter Skelter was the right thing to do. Purity in its purest form. But Manson had also been a musician with a wonderful voice, and musicians tended to be graced with some level of sensitivity. Before Lucas could reveal he was merely being the devil's advocate, he was met with blank stares from fellow students and a concerned look from his professor, but little else. And he'd felt like an idiot for never realizing before that moment that most people only cared about their own trivial problems. The rest of the universe could fuck right off.

What he'd known deep down then but never truly registered until this morning was that good and evil were just two shades of grey in an overcast world. And he now leaned toward the latter. Always had. He was part of the remaining twenty percent. Pure and unfiltered.

He was the beast under the bridge that couldn't possibly be human but is. The lifer with no remorse. The man who murdered his wife in a "crime of passion" but secretly fantasized for years about gutting her and sewing her offal into an ascot.

This revelation made him realize a few key things about life.

It was perfectly acceptable to kick a feral alley cat or two, just make sure to avoid the neighbor's prissy pussy since it's a beloved pet. Cuteness, a name, a knitted sweater on a poodle made it off limits. Pets were pretty, petty things.

There was nothing inherently wrong about stealing a candy bar, then a comic book, then some CDs, then pirating a few recently released flicks for good measure, then upgrading to a new pair of fancy pleather shoes. It didn't matter that he had the money to buy anything his heart desired. It was about the thrill. The thrill of pulling one leg of a used pair of pantyhose over his head and holding up a corner liquor store just for kicks. The clerk would never know it was just a squirt gun in his jacket pocket (if in fact it was), and Lucas would only get away with a few hundred bucks, but it would be worth it for the rush of blood into his needy schlong.

It was completely normal to fuck the head cheerleader, so long as he made sure to pull out in time to avoid getting her pregnant, or pay for abortion number three if need be. Maybe it'd be better to consider anal instead, because then the worst outcome would probably be finding a fully intact kernel of corn dangling at the head of his dick like a fresh wart. Hell, he even figured it was A-OK to let the quarterback suck him off after. After all, playing football made a man hungry and lonely and in need some flavorful lovin'. Nothing wrong with a kink or three so long as the outside world remained ignorant to what you were doing behind closed doors. Why waste time with vanilla when Baskin-Robbins was within your reach?

And really, who hadn't bribed their AP History teacher in high school with carefully-placed child pornography so they could get accepted into some Ivy League school on the other side of the country? And was it so wrong to realize he didn't want to stray too far from his mother's teat after all, that he'd slept through all of his important classes the first semester because he was too tired from boring frat parties he hadn't attended anyway? Elephant Walk, Soggy Biscuit, Greek Flamethrower, they were all old hat. So fucking passé.

Did he have nonconsensual intercourse with a buzzed coed? Did it matter? If she didn't remember and there were no witnesses and he didn't care, did it actually happen?

Lucas was acutely aware of his privilege as a rich white male. He was thankful for it, and he had sure as hell used it to his advantage.

But now, the morning after Halloween, he was wondering if any of this had ever really been his life. Was it somehow prophesized before his birth that he would end up as this new man today? Had he ever really been Lucas? Or was Lucas just a character in a dream he'd made up to convince himself he was normal? Well, relatively normal.

He wasn't complaining. In fact, he wanted to know who he had to thank for this fresh transformation. He owed them a fancy dinner at the very least.

Grady Sullivan spoke to him in his head. There was no one else to speak to. He had some very profound things to say to Lucas:

Understand this, friend. I am the shadow that hides within other shadows, the dangerous man you'd never notice because you're too busy patting yourself on the back for throwing a dollar in his cup, the scratching sound outside your kitchen window while you try to scrape those pesky leftovers off of your fine china, the wriggling half-worm in your half-eaten apple, the close friend you don't actually know very well at all, the laugh in the next room that you decide was your imagination because you're the only one in the building (aren't you?).

I am you now, and you are me. We are essentially we.

Are we clear?

This wasn't some form of schizophrenia. It was sheer lucidity. Would it be fair to lock him up just because he wanted to quench his thirst with the milky ichor of supposed virgins? Because he yearned to glue HIV-infested razors to a belt, whip said belt above his head like a helicopter's blades, and toss it into an overpopulated playground in the center of some upscale outdoor shopping mall just to see which little brat would take the bait?

They'd have to catch him first. But that wouldn't be easy. Not even a little. He was a fictional character. A promotional poster. He was created by ill minds, marketed to the malleable youth, and somehow morphed into a box office smash. Killers made a killing in good ole Hol-ly-wood. Maybe some of the later *Emancipation Day* sequels hadn't broken any records, but even legends needed to be humbled from time to time. It was the kind of thing that built character.

And then another philosophical conundrum entered his head. Which came first—the movie or the killing spree? Death inspired death inspired art. Anything could be art if the person who created it decided it was art. *Mother Mary with the Holy Child Jesus Christ* by Adolf Hitler? Art. Shit in a glass? Art. Eviscerated family? Art. Silicone camel toe? There was pattern, a design, and it couldn't be overstated.

He didn't even look remotely the same anymore. No one would ever recognize him. No one would ever see him coming. He was a brand new Lucas. No. A new *Grady*. New body, shared mind. It was his temple and he'd worship it however the hell he wanted.

Lucas Lane was a lie that had been perpetuated for far too long.

Grady Sullivan was now the only reality.

He knew what he needed to do next.

And those on his list would surely suffer dearly.

CHAPTER TEN

BEFORE THIS MORNING, Edgar Cotton had never been able to lick his own testicles. It's not that he'd actually attempted it, but he was certain he'd fantasized about it at some point. Edgar firmly believed most or perhaps even all males would perform self-fellatio at least once if they were flexible enough. Now, in a peculiar dream that felt frighteningly real, Edgar was more or less satisfying this urge. Because he could.

The only problem: his body was now squat, small, black, and furry. A flat, bug-eyed face and a curly tail.

Edgar was a pug.

Though it was strange, it certainly made relative sense considering his chosen costume for Hannah's party. No matter, he thought, because he'd experienced much stranger dreams than this one. He had tried, but miserably failed, to wipe from his memory the time he dreamt about his now-deceased grandmother dressed like a poor man's version of Sade, singing "Sweetest Taboo." Shriveled kneecaps, varicose veins bulging from her flabby thighs like blue raspberry licorice, a cheap dark wig slicked back and offset on her balding, scabrous head. If anything could make a penis shrink a few inches, it was a dream like that one.

But Edgar kept licking and licking and it basically felt good. Not as good as if performed by a professional, and he'd certainly had enough experience with ladies of the night to know the difference, but he cut himself some slack because it was only his first attempt. He suddenly passed gas and it startled him. He winced at the scent of his own flatulence. It was not the familiar scent he ignored on any other given morning. It fell somewhere between sweet potatoes and raw fish. He wasn't completely appalled by it, either.

Edgar grew bored with his grooming antics and decided to waddle over to Jack's room. He had always prided himself in waking his rich boy roommate in the most obnoxious ways possible, especially the morning after a big party, using such tactics as blaring David Hasselhoff's *Night Rocker* album, crashing two metal garbage can lids together alongside a radio broadcast of *O Fortuna*, and releasing a box full of baby crickets he purchased from the pet store, justifying that they would have been fed to somebody's bearded dragon if he hadn't liberated them. At least they'd had a slim chance of survival hopping around Jack's room.

In Edgar's mind, the greater you pranked someone, the greater the love you felt for that person. To be purely kind to any friend, especially one as close as Jack, was a wretched insult of the highest order.

Edgar huffed and puffed down the hallway, seeing the apartment from a much different perspective than normal. He realized, but ultimately didn't care, just how filthy the floor was. He spied a crumb, something that looked like a popcorn kernel, then pressed his face against it and sniffed it while making some strange distorted honking sound. He sucked the kernel into his mouth and chomped it. It was stale, old, flavorless. He loved it.

He carried on down the hallway until he reached Jack's door. It was closed. Normally this would not be much of a deterrent, as Jack was not known for locking his door. On any normal day Edgar typically had opposable thumbs capable of turning a knob, but this dream he was in the midst of had obviously put him in a bit of a pickle. He did what any pug in his situation would do. He scratched at the door while releasing a series of barks that sounded like his throat had been muffled with a pair of gym socks. He hopped around in clumsy circles, continuing the barking ritual. A drowsy "What the fuck?" came from behind the door and Edgar snickered and snorted to himself. Even though this was a dream, it was still great to get that frustrated reaction out of his roommate. Getting Jack's goat never failed to bring a smile to Edgar's face, and it felt just as good now as it did in real life. It was going to be an even greater payoff when he got to the real part of the prank.

A few heavy, clumsy footsteps and Jack opened the door, his exploding hair sculpted by artistically talented pillows, his morning wood almost escaping through the fly of his checkered boxers, barely saved by the button. He rubbed his eyes, grumbled a few obscenities, and looked down. Edgar lifted his leg and peed directly on Jack's bare leg, thinking this act didn't really matter since it was a dream. There was no law, and there were no repercussions in the Land of Nod.

Jack leaped back and howled in disgust, possibly inventing a few curse words in the process. He looked down both sides of the hallway, his face frozen in rage. "Fuck! Edgar! Get out here right fucking now! Where the hell did this goddamned dog come from?" He stomped down the hall toward Edgar's room, shaking his leg off to the side as he stumbled, adding even more grime to the floor, filth that would remain until the end of time or until they moved and their landlord replaced the carpet. Jack reached Edgar's room and threw the door open. "Aw, come on . . . where the hell are you? Goddamned prick."

Edgar cackled. He rolled on his side. "Gotcha, man! Oh, hell . . . the look on your face is priceless." Jack turned to look at Edgar, and Edgar noticed his friend was wearing a brand new expression. A silent, contorted mask, his jaw drooping as if he wanted to collect any stray dust bunnies that might have been hopping across the floor.

It was then that Edgar, in the back of his mind, realized there was a chance he might not be dreaming after all. It didn't register as reality, though. It hovered off to the side, and Edgar wondered if it was possible to experience the sensation of doubt within the confines of a dream.

"It was funny, right?" Edgar said, the tone of his voice now heavy with worry.

Jack stared at Edgar and kneeled down. He cracked a smile, as if he was certain this was all a clever magic trick. One for the history books. He laughed uncomfortably. "That's a really wicked trick, Edgar. Didn't even know you were practicing ventriloquism. You still gotta clean up the piss, though, asshole. We'll lose our fucking deposit."

"Jack?" Edgar's voice was a raspy whisper now. "What the hell is going on?"

Jack's body jerked. "Hey, bud . . . can you come out now? I'm over it. This is getting a little creepy, dude."

"I'm. Right. Here."

Jack crawled closer to Edgar's face, almost close enough to kiss him. "Say that again. What'd you give this little guy, huh? Chunky peanut butter? Better not have been my goddamned gourmet stuff. I swear I'll—"

"Jack. Shut up for a second, will you?"

Jack's eyes revealed that he knew there was no peanut butter nor any other consumable substance in the dog's mouth, that the words synced up perfectly with the mouth's motions. They were both silent for a few moments. Jack looked deep into Edgar's eyes. Edgar whimpered to try and make the situation less awkward.

"I'm scared, man," Edgar said. "Really fucking freaked."

Jack crawled backward a few paces and pushed himself into a sitting position. He rubbed his fingers through his thick hair, pulling it back until it stretched his skin and gave him a slight facelift. "Yeah . . . yeah. Okay. Join the club, dude. Are you sure you didn't slip me something really bad last night? Or maybe that was my own fault, but—"

"Shouldn't I be asking you the same thing? I swear . . . tell me this isn't happening. Oh, crap, please tell me this is just a really bad dream and I'm gonna wake up and hopefully some insanely hot chick is going to be lying next to me. Is that too much to ask?" Edgar was having trouble fooling himself. He could feel his dewclaws getting caught in the Berber carpet. He felt like he needed to shit and realized he was too short to reach the toilet. He wondered if Jack would be willing to let him outside to go do his business.

"Oh, man. Give me a second to think."

"Hell . . . it wouldn't even have to be Beth. I'd even take someone like . . . like Trish Stratton if it meant that was the worst thing that actually happened last night."

Jack made a disgusted face at this remark. Edgar meant business if he was bringing that beast Trish in the mix.

"Okay," Jack said, closing his eyes, apparently in deep thought, "so what the hell do we do now?"

Before Edgar could answer, the phone rang.

CHAPTER ELEVEN

KEEPING HER EYES closed was not good enough. The light still bled through Kat's eyelids, creating a stretched canvas effect. Where the hell was her eye mask? Probably lying atop one of the many piles of clothes on the floor, just out of convenient reach. She certainly wasn't going to go look for it right now.

Where was Jack? She vaguely recalled him driving her home, making sure she arrived safely. Her car was probably still parked four blocks down from Hannah's house. She blindly patted around the bed, hoping to feel Jack's sleeping body there. She was only mildly disappointed. She knew it was the ultimate long shot. She'd have to call him later, get him to drive her back to the hills to pick up her car.

She pressed her face down into her pillow, trying to block out the blaring sun entering her room. She felt the cotton of her pillowcase sticking to the thick crust in her eyes and it was like Mr. Sandman had taken a sloppy dump on her face and left it to dry. She moaned and wished she had the power to turn back time and sleep just a few more hours, or maybe even a full day the way she was feeling. She didn't have to work today—thankfully Benji's Boutique was closed on Sundays, but she'd definitely call in if she still felt like this tomorrow. If her boss gave her a guilt trip, she'd just quit. The wonderful world of retail would keep spinning without her indifferent contribution. Besides, it was about time for a change. A fresh start. Something drastic.

She pulled away from the pillow and felt a quick tear and a sharp pain on the edge of her eyelid. The sting woke her up better than any alarm clock could have. She squinted at the pillow, which now had one of her eyelashes attached to it. Her actual eyelash. Kat would never have stooped so low as to attach a fake one to her face. Not even for Halloween. That would have just been tacky.

A small bit of scabby flesh was attached to the fine hair. Small droplets of blood.

Kat felt dizzy.

The pillow looked like it was drunkenly winking at her. Kat tossed it to the other side of her room. It crashed into her vanity, toppling the miniature cities of makeup. The decibel level of her screams ebbed and flowed, close to reaching the tantrum stage. She tried to calm herself down, but couldn't seem to do any better than severe hyperventilation. Why the hell had something so small hurt so damned much? And why the hell had it even happened?

She applied pressure to her eye and it didn't help at all, just added more to the stickiness. When she attempted to get out of bed, the sheets clung to her body and for a moment she wondered if someone had snuck into her room last night and drowned her bed in maple syrup. Trick or fucking treat. She ran to the vanity mirror, her sheets hanging like a loose toga, and went completely silent when she finally got a good look at herself.

Kat had fallen asleep in her costume last night because she had been a little too wasted to bother with anything but sleep. But this was not just a costume anymore. This was . . . something else.

She wanted to scream again, but her throat wouldn't let her anymore. It was raw and dry and needed a break or at least a refreshing beverage to soothe it, so the stress surged right into her brain. She wanted to faint, but she felt weightless. If she attempted to let her body fall, the laws of gravity would fail her and she would float to the ceiling and stick to it like a Wacky WallWalker. She wanted to look away from her reflection, but couldn't. She was the car accident she always secretly wished she would witness, but it was supposed to have been someone else's gross inconvenience.

Without tearing her gaze from the horror in the mirror, she reached for her phone.

———◆———

Less than an hour later, Jack was there. He sat at the opposite end of the kitchen table from Kat, the cheap plastic chair turned around the incorrect direction, his legs squatting around the edges. Kat absently thought he must have been raised to think this was the correct way to sit because she couldn't ever remember seeing him sit otherwise. Not at his house, not at any restaurant that had moveable seats, even back in high school, no matter how much teachers pointlessly chastised him for it. He must have hated it when a classroom was only equipped with chairs that had desks attached to them.

Jack was in deep thought. Not much different than most other days they spent time together. This brief mundane moment almost fooled Kat into thinking things were okay, but then she looked down at Edgar—the *new* Edgar, lying on his side, his gigantic pink tongue plopped out the side of his mouth. He was breathing heavily, as if he had just attempted a marathon and gave up halfway through. She couldn't really blame him. It was close to 90 degrees outside and rising. The heat was making her stickier by the second.

"You know," Kat said. "I'm not supposed to have dogs in here."

"Bite me," Edgar said. "I think eviction is the least of your problems, don't you?"

"Oh, what the hell do you know? At least you're not—"

"Guys," Jack said. "Cool it. Serious talk now. What are we going to do?"

"Well," Edgar said, "I was thinking about checking out the hydrant down the street. See what all the fuss is about."

Jack stared at him, his glare shaping into a finely pointed dart. "I'm glad to see you're taking this so goddamned seriously. Maybe you're perfectly fine with your current situation, but . . . I mean— look at poor Kat. Just look at her!"

Kat sobbed and heaved and shook and she just wanted Jack to come hold her. He looked so normal and wonderful that a simple hug might have made her temporarily forget about her condition. But Jack wouldn't budge. He was afraid. Kat could see it in his eyes, those eyes that would barely look at her straight on, and it made her afraid of her disgusting self. Jack probably thought if he hugged her he'd catch what she has, that some rotten piece of her would slide off and attach to his hand. He'd shake it and scream like a prepubescent girl but it wouldn't come loose no matter how much he wished it to be so. It'd crawl up his arms, grow on him, become a part of him, and eat him away until he was nothing but a walking pile of rot. Just like her. At least they'd have something special in common. Something physically intimate to share.

But Kat knew there would be no chance for a tender moment. She was sure Jack thought she was a living sewer, a horrendous ghoul. He thought she was ugly and he was absolutely right.

"Aw, fucking hell," Jack said. "I'm sorry, Kat. I didn't mean to . . ."

Kat waved at him but did not try to make eye contact. She didn't know if she'd ever be able to again. She was already afraid of what she'd seen in Jack's eyes. She didn't want to know if it could possibly get worse.

Jack removed his glasses, rubbed his eyes with such force that Kat was concerned they might burst like grapes. "Kat, this is so fucked. We've got to get you to a hospital. Now. Maybe someone there can—"

"No," Kat said. "No way. I don't . . . No. I don't like hospitals."

"Are you fucking kidding me? This isn't just a bad rash or a little acne breakout. A natural cream and a little TLC aren't going to make this go away."

"Okay, fine. Great. So go ahead and take me to a hospital. Then once they figure out they've got something rare on their hands and they get Nobel Prize-inspired delusions of grandeur, they'll decide to lock me up in some lab and prod me and study me, then let me die and do a fucking autopsy on my corpse so they can finally figure out what caused this. Sounds like an awesome plan, Jack. Wish I would have thought of it myself."

"Kat, I think you've seen too many movies."

"The answer is no."

"Does this mean I have to go see a veterinarian?" Edgar asked.

Jack turned to Edgar. "Really, man? Can you just cut it out and be real for once? Think about someone other than yourself." Edgar hung his head in pitiful doglike shame. Jack returned his attention to Kat. "Look, we can't just sit around and do nothing. This situation isn't getting any better. What if it gets worse? What if you . . . "

"What if I what?" Kat asked the question even though she knew the answer. Even though she knew Jack had no intention of finishing his thought.

"Kat, please."

"I don't know. None of it sounds any good. Can't we just wait? Just a little bit? Maybe it'll wear off."

Jack blew out a deep breath. "I don't think it will. I understand you're terrified, but we're not waiting too long, okay? We can't. There's got to be some explanation for this. Something logical."

"Hey, Mr. Spock," Edgar said, "you do realize logic flew the coop along with the Great Pumpkin last night, don't you, bro?"

"But, like, there's still a reason this is happening. A cause. We can't realistically do anything to change this before we figure that out, right? Start with the source, then go from there."

"There's something else I'm confused about," Kat said. Her voice came out sounding like a frog in a blender. She looked at the cabinet above the sink. Her honey bear was in there. She wanted to grab it, squeeze out some sugary goodness, let it soothe her throat. "Why didn't you change, Jack? I'm not saying I wish you did or that *you* wish you did, but . . . "

"No. I know. I'm a lucky motherfucker and I have zero clue why I'm not, uh . . . wolfed out?"

"Maybe it's because you've gotta wait until a full moon," Edgar said. Kat looked at Jack, worried. It was the most sensible thing Edgar had said all morning. Maybe ever.

"Well," Jack said, his voice less confident now, "you could be right. That's part of what we need to figure out, though, yeah? We need to get in touch with some people from last night. Go back to—"

"—Hannah's house." Kat and Jack had always been able to complete each other's sentences, and today was no exception. The living, breathing cancer she had become had not stifled that connection. Kat felt temporary comfort in this bond. Too temporary.

"It's as good a place to start as any," Jack said. "Let's motor. We can't sit around and waste any more time."

Edgar responded with a fart. "All right . . . to the Mystery Machine, I guess."

———◆———

It was a strange mid-Autumn afternoon. The past week full of Santa Ana winds refused to give up the ghost. The heat was oppressive and humid, a thick, seasonal paste that needed to be waded through and shoveled out of the way. Jack was in the driver's seat of his '85 Volvo.

Kat rode shotgun. She wore baggy jeans and a hoodie despite the unbearable weather. It prevented her from becoming a spectacle. Edgar's two front paws were propped on the left windowsill, his head catching as much breeze as possible. He barked playfully at passersby. The people on the sidewalk barely acknowledged him. All was normal in their version of the world. Halloween was over, and they were already heading to the department store to score some candy and check out the Christmas displays.

An EDM version of "Achy Breaky Heart" seeped from the stereo and no one seemed to mind. An abomination such as this seemed about right for these dark times. Life was twisted and might never unravel into normalcy ever again.

"Holy shit!" Kat's body jerked at Jack's exclamation. She stared at him, trying to contain her heart attack. His eyes were like a child's after figuring out 2+2 did not equal 3. "I think I know what caused this. Or who caused this, I guess."

"What is it, big boy?" Edgar asked, whipping his head back into the car. "Don't keep us in suspense."

"Cosmo's."

"Fuck me. You're right."

"What?" Kat asked. "Why do you think . . . oh. Yeah. Duh."

"I don't know why I didn't think of it before," Jack said. "That's got to be the link, right? You got your costume there, so did Ed. It'd explain why I didn't change, wouldn't it?"

"I guess so," Kat said. "But why and how?"

"Search me. We'll figure that out eventually. But let's see if Hannah has any ideas. We can compare notes, figure out who else went to Cosmo's, see if they're having their own set of problems."

"Hannah wouldn't know a dick from a pickle," Edgar said.

"Shut up, asshole," Jack said. "You're just pissed because she wouldn't go out with you."

"No, Beth's still pissed because Hannah wouldn't go out with me. She wouldn't even let me apologize last night."

"Oh. Ha. Yeah. Bad form, man."

"Still have no idea how she found out."

"Christ, Ed," Kat said, "does that even matter right now?"

Edgar tried to shrug, but apparently a pug could not shrug.

"Oh, no," Kat said.

"What?" Jack asked.

"Hannah got her costume there, too."

"Shit."

The Volvo entered the on-ramp to the 101 and they headed toward the hills.

CHAPTER TWELVE

KAT LEANED HER head out the window, just enough to let the wind blow her hair into a maddening mess. It didn't matter if it looked good anymore. A nice 'do was the least of her worries. The crisp air slightly stung the dry, chapped scabs on her face and soothed the fresh, wet wounds, but she pretended not to notice. Jack and Edgar were babbling on and on about first-person shooter games, sporting events, urinating with an erection. Guy stuff. At least they had something to temporarily get their minds off the current situation. They were doing a good job of pretending everything was okay. She was not fortunate enough to have such escapism.

They were on Mullholland now, on their way to Hannah's. Though the winding streets in the hills were much less threatening in the light of day, were far safer to navigate with the sun's guidance, Kat felt no relief. And, ultimately, she didn't care. She welcomed danger, wanted to at least share a polite conversation with Death, see what he had to offer. It had to be better than the current hand she had been dealt.

She let her eyes wander off toward the canyons, toward the side of the road, which was occasionally unprotected by guardrails. Wide open spaces just begging for a free fall. Even the guardrails that *were* there seemed like a mere formality.

She quietly removed her seatbelt. She wanted to feel free. She wanted options. The scenery zipped by like a videotape in fast forward. Endless blades of dead or dying brush. A middle-aged couple walking their dog. A darting squirrel. A discarded shoe. For a moment she wished Jack would lose control of the steering wheel, perhaps speed up an extra 10 MPH upon reaching Dead Man's Curve. The Volvo would hit the curve hard, tumble over the side, and fly high for a moment, a stunt car in a nail-biting scene from an action film. Kat would be thrown from the car, then crushed beneath its weight. Jack would survive, perhaps Edgar as well if he were lucky. But she would become one with the weeds. Her blood would mix with the dirt in a coagulated mess. She would be fodder for the creatures of Laurel Canyon.

But she knew Jack would never come close to putting her in danger. Hell, he would never even risk Edgar's life. For all his flaws, for all his asshole-ish ways, Edgar was like a brother to Jack. Though, perhaps now he was closer to a pet. How things change.

"Hey, Kat, you okay?" Jack asked. "We're almost there."

"Hmm?"

"You alright?"

"Yup. Five by five."

"What the fuck does that mean?" Edgar asked.

Kat didn't answer. She shut him out, shut out everything except her wish to cease being.

———————◆———————

Kat winced as she pressed the doorbell to Hannah's house. Even that small action hurt her finger like hell. The once-white bell now had a dark mark smeared on it. She had to remove her hoodie because she was afraid of heatstroke, but she wished she hadn't left it in the car. Even with a thin tee on, she still felt worse than naked now. She would rather have been her normal self, without a stitch of clothing on her body, doing drunken cartwheels in front of elderly Republicans in a Deep South dive bar than have had the current version of herself even somewhat exposed.

"Edgar," Jack said, "I really wish you hadn't shed all over my backseat. That's going to be a bitch to clean."

"Hey, what do you want from me? I can't help it. I need a good solid brushing and I sure as hell can't do it myself."

"You're fooling yourself if you think I'm going to—"

"Come on . . . It's not like the upholstery is in primo shape."

Kat shushed them sternly and achieved relative silence as a result. Jack patted her softly on the back, an apparent apology without words. The contact shocked her. She was grateful for even the slightest attempt at a touch. It made her feel almost human.

The doors were huge and ivory white, solid oak glaciers laced with gold trim. Edgar scratched at one of them. Light footsteps pattered on the other side, then a pause, and the door opened without so much as a creak. It was Hannah's mother, looking all done up like an extra from a *Dynasty* rerun. Her nose was stolen from a witch, her hair from Ivana Trump, her makeup from Tammy Faye. She was wearing sunglasses indoors. She'd likely had her own version of a wild Halloween night, but she still pulled it together rather well.

Kat avoided making eye contact with her.

"Oh, hello Katherine," she said, barely pulling her sunglasses down. Forests of red veins spread across her sclera. "Haven't seen you in a while, dear."

"Hi Mrs. Harper." Hannah's mother didn't seem to acknowledge the horror of Kat's new look, glossed past it as if she had looked this way from birth. This came as no surprise to Kat. The debauchery that had occurred under Mrs. Harper's nose, in her own house, sometimes when she was home and even occasionally in the same room, was not quantifiable. She wouldn't have noticed Hannah snorting a line of coke if it had been off her own tit, much less bat an eye upon seeing her daughter's best friend looking like she had been in some sort of horrible accident. And she wouldn't have cared much either. Hannah had told Kat stories about things her mother had done, things that probably should have been kept secret but weren't, nights that should have probably been erased from history. "Is Hannah home?"

"Yes, I believe she's still out in the pool with that . . . ahem . . . boy." Her voice quivered when speaking the last word. Kat presumed Mrs. Harper was referring to Jonah, the gladiator from last night. The top half of the older woman's eyes flickered with a strange lust, and Kat suddenly imagined her rushing off to her room and unearthing a 9-inch dildo she referred to as "Brutus." It wouldn't be the first time Mrs. Harper had fantasized about one of her daughter's boy-toys. Kat would have bet what little money she had that at least one of those fantasies had become reality. She wasn't sure if she found that revolting or impressive.

"She certainly is spending a lot of time in the water today. She's going to get wrinkles. I don't know when that girl is ever going to learn." Mrs. Harper stepped aside and let them in. "Ximena just made some freshly-brewed peach iced tea. Help yourself."

Ximena. A name Kat had heard many times, a name attached to a person she had never seen but had to have existed. In the Harper house, the help apparently hid in the shadows when guests arrived.

"Peach schnapps would be better," Edgar said, "but I just might take you up on that anyway." Mrs. Harper nodded and cooed, as if a chunky black pug speaking to her was an everyday occurrence. If ignorance was bliss, Mrs. Harper must have been one happy bitch. Kat thought for a moment this could be just another piece of the puzzle. Perhaps no one aside from those who had attended the party were even aware something had changed. They were trapped in a vortex that could not be viewed by outside eyes.

Or, the more likely option, Mrs. Harper couldn't have given two shits to charity.

"I'm off to meet some friends for a late brunch and shopping," Mrs. Harper said. "Will you be a darling and tell Hannah I won't be back until . . . well, I'm not quite sure. Will you please just tell her?"

"Sure," Kat said. "Of course."

The house was spick-and-span. It was as if a party had never even occurred within this building, like the entire filthy aura of Halloween had been absorbed into the clean cream walls and was now staining offensive images on the sheetrock. Had Hannah cleaned this all herself? Had she convinced her harem of strapping young men to help her? Had the mysterious Ximena done the dirty work? No . . . it had to have been professional services if it was done this quickly and this perfectly. Why do the work if you could afford to have it done for you, and at a moment's notice?

Even though Kat had just been in this house last night and had spent more time here than she could count over the last few years, it still took the three of them a while to make their way toward the back to find the pool. They were momentarily lost in a hallway that turned out to be a coat closet, and then they headed down a staircase that somehow sent them to a slightly higher level of the house, ending at an open space that led to nowhere. A walkway that ended without a railing or a wall, just a drop. Not safe for children. Kat peered over the edge and saw they were now just above the foyer. She had never been up here before, didn't even know this part of the home existed. Hannah's house sometimes felt like an Escher lithograph come to life in the form of a posh resort.

They retraced some of their steps and Kat briefly worried that they might run into a Minotaur at some point. It wouldn't have been the strangest thing they'd seen today. Jack made a quick stop in the bathroom because they might not be able to find it again on the way out. Kat and Edgar waited outside, awkwardly and inadvertently listening to Jack go tinkle. An act so mundane that Kat almost found it attractive.

Eventually they arrived at the giant wall of windows that led to the backyard. The sun was a spotlight controlled by a real dick of a technician.

At the pool, Jonah was sprawled across a teak chaise lounge, his body sinking into a mauve cushion. He was almost nude save for a loincloth and a pair of blue tanning goggles. He still looked his normal, statue-like self. There was no sign of Hannah, but they heard sounds of splashing near the surface of the pool.

"Hey, I think that's—" Jack could barely squeak this out before Hannah surfaced. She whipped her soaked red hair back and forth a few times and the water droplets seemed to explode in slow motion. She was topless, her pale, slightly freckled breasts beacons to a world of unknown pleasures. No one blinked because this was certainly not the first time they'd seen Hannah's hand puppets. The right mix of cocktail and crystal and out they came like carolers at Christmas. She looked at Jack and barely acknowledged him, probably because he looked the same as always. Then she turned her attention to Edgar and didn't seem to realize it was Edgar, but made kissy noises because she simply died whenever she saw a dog she found adorable. If Hannah could eat a dog for breakfast just to love it more, Kat believed she would do so at least once a week. Strangely, she had no furry pets of her own. Never had.

"Stop being such an annoying bitch, Hannah," Edgar said.

"Ooo-kay," Hannah said. Her eyes widened as she looked at Kat. Her lips parted, and for the first time in her life she had absolutely nothing to say. But Kat knew what Hannah was thinking, and it sucked her soul right out of her body. The girl who had told some of the tallest tales imaginable couldn't lie to Kat with her eyes. Even Hannah was not that talented.

Hannah flopped her full body up onto the concrete and revealed her bottom half. Her fishy side hit the ground with a wet slap. There was no seam. Not anymore. The tail was real now. It blended smoothly into Hannah's flesh. Her emerald scales glistened in the sun, and the salty scent of a chlorine-treated sea wafted over Kat. In some sick way, Hannah was somehow even more beautiful than before. She was a sailor's fantasy made fetishistic flesh.

No one said a word and no one needed to. Kat supposed this was what everyone expected—she certainly had, but that made the reveal no less shocking. She could hear Edgar quietly humming "Under the Sea" next to her and she shoved him with her foot. He grunted and headed toward the flawlessly green yard adjacent to the pool, grumbling incoherently. Kat turned away from Hannah, hugging her own rotting body tight.

Jonah awoke from his sunbathing slumber and approached the group. He looked like he had been trying and failing to recover from a really bad night that had turned into an even worse morning. Probably an accurate assessment, though his morning couldn't have been worse than the morning some of them were having. This was more than an average hangover. His bronzed body smelled like coconut, and Kat thought for a moment that she'd really like to play Tic Tac Toe on his six pack. As if he'd let her. She wouldn't have even had a chance beforehand. It would take a lot of liquor and perhaps a considerable payoff for him to let her touch those abs now. She felt guilty for even looking at them.

Jonah pulled Jack aside and whispered to him, but not quietly enough. Kat could still hear. "Hey, man. I don't get it. Hannah and I . . . we tried to, you know, like . . . do it earlier. I thought I was just still high, but I'm not. I swear. We tried to boink and I can't find the hole, man. It's, like, not there or something. She's changed. Somebody's yankin' my chain, right? Aw, man, what the fuck?" Kat could smell alcohol exuding from his pores. Hair of the dog in full force.

"I don't think I really need to know that, bud," Jack said. He politely removed Jonah's hand from his shirt. Kat could tell Jack was doing his best to inch away from him.

"I ate a hot dog this morning," Jonah said. "At least I think it was a hot dog. Aw, geez, I hope so. I'm really sick now. Why did I do that, you know? Who knows where that thing had been? I can't stop going, man. Every fifteen minutes I've gotta make a mad dash for the shitter."

"Uh, my previous statement still stands. I don't know. Lips and assholes, dude. That shit ain't good for you."

"Have you seen my buddy Ken? Do you know him?" Jack shook his head. Jonah's hand was attached to Jack's shirt again. "I tried calling his house, but I can't get ahold of him. I thought I . . . thought I saw him this morning, but . . . I don't know. Must've been mistaken. The fucker. Figures he would bail when I need him most."

Kat tried to get Jack's attention, to pull him away from Jonah, but Jonah had a firm grip on Jack for the time being, both literally and figuratively.

Edgar was now out in the perfectly trimmed yard, taking a massive dump. It wasn't the first time Kat had seen him defecate in public. He was grinning in the purely dumb way that only a dog can, balanced on three legs, his fourth dangling and making him looking like an inept gymnast during his first attempt at using parallel bars. If it helped Edgar squeeze it out easier, more power to him.

"Kat," Hannah said, finally rediscovering the power of verbal communication. "Oh my fucking God. Come here, babe." Kat broke out of her trance a bit. She had expected Hannah to stretch her arms out to offer one of her signature ginormous hugs, but she did not.

Kat sat by the side of the pool near Hannah, with a buffer zone approximately the size of an average human. She got the hint. Any attempts at comfort were futile.

She removed her shoes, dipped her feet into the cool water. Her leprous leg went limp. It was the first relief she'd felt all day.

"You poor thing," Hannah continued. Her eyes dampened. Despite the lack of physical comfort, her concern was sincere. Of course it was. She and Kat had been BFFs too long to let even something as insane as this situation get in the way of their sisterly love. Granted, at least some of Hannah's tears were probably due to her own transformation, but Kat understood. She felt guilty for thinking her friend would ever even consider disowning her, even in freak form. "Nobody deserves this, least of all you."

They both let loose more tears, but did so quietly. There was an unspoken law now. They had to remain strong. Otherwise, they had absolutely no chance of crossing back into any sort of normalcy.

Kat's voice dropped to a whisper. "Jack's trying to get me to go to a doctor. I can't, though. Hannah, I just—"

"Oh, God, no," Hannah's volume now matched Kat's. "Of course not, hon. You mean—He doesn't know, does he?"

Kat shook her head. She wiped away tears that were wetting her rotten side, making it stink, making it sticky. Something burst at the top of her cheekbone and oozed onto her fingers. Out of the corner of her eye she looked in Hannah's direction, mortified, but Hannah was facing forward, wiping away her own tears. Kat quickly smeared the white viscous fluid on her pants. It left a wet spot on the fabric.

After they were both able to regain their cool, Kat asked, "Do you have any idea what happened?"

Hannah wrinkled her nose. "Damn. No. I was hoping you guys would know."

"Jack has a theory. I dunno. We're hoping you can help." Kat told Hannah about the likelihood of the costume shop's involvement, and Hannah seemed reasonably convinced. It was the only lead anyone had, but it was a fairly reasonable one.

"Well, maybe we can—"

"Hannah, what am I going to do?" Kat's inner strength crumbled once again. She put her hand to her mouth in an attempt to compose herself, not realizing it was her damaged hand until she felt the jagged, peeling flesh against her untainted lips. It scratched at her like a hangnail that had been left to grow far too long. "What are *we* going to do?"

"We need to all go down there and confront those dicks. At least find out what the hell they did to us, *how* they did it so we can figure out how to undo it. I mean . . . if we just show up, they won't be expecting it. They must think we're stupid. We'll fuck those fuckers up if we have to." Kat raised her eyebrow at Hannah, and Hannah sighed in response. "I mean, I guess I can't really go, but the rest of you can. And you can take Jonah if you want. Once he sobers up anyway. He needs to pull his damned weight somehow. He's been fucking useless this morning."

"I suppose we could use some muscle."

"What we need to do," Jack said from behind Kat, startling her. He was apparently free from Jonah's ramblings now. Kat spun her body around and peered through Jack's legs. Jonah had returned to the chaise lounge. He was curled in a ball, clutching his stomach, practically already napping again. "What we need to do is track down anyone else from the party who we know for sure got their costumes at Cosmo's, then head over there in large numbers. We have to find out if it's their fault and if they can change you all back."

"Isn't that what I just said?" Hannah asked.

"Dunno," Jack said. "Your boyfriend there had me a little occupied."

"Okay," Hannah said. "Well, I know a few other people for sure went to Cosmo's. Carey Lane and . . . shit, what's his brother's name?"

"Lucas," Kat said.

"Yes! Him. God, I hate that asshole."

"You and every other woman on Planet Earth," Jack said.

"Don't even get me started," Hannah said. "Let's see . . . Sidney Gates definitely got his costume there. I saw him when I picked mine up. Um . . . maybe Bryce Patterson? Not sure. Have to check."

"Great. I'm sort of afraid to even bring this up based on what his costume was, but add Freddie Wright to that list. Can anyone say Jurassic fucking Park? I'm sure there's more. Hannah, can you make a few calls while we're gone? I want to head over to Wade Garrison's place. I'm sure he'd be willing to help. Carey's probably there anyway."

"Yeah. Yeah, of course."

"That's a good enough plan to start with, I guess," Kat said. "Go get Edgar. We need to make sure we're all on the same page."

"I would if I had any clue where that little shit went."

———— • • ————

Edgar finished relieving himself, kicked his hind legs through the grass a few times, and wandered toward the guesthouse behind the pool. He heard a curious noise inside and assumed it was a cat. Hoped it was, actually, because that was quickly becoming his nature. Far be it from him to ignore his natural enemy.

He waddled to the doorway, peeked his head through, and did not find a frightened feline. Instead, he found the last thing in the world he expected.

A baby.

A baby dressed in an inappropriately sexy outfit. Sitting crisscross applesauce, turned away from the door and facing the far corner of the room. She didn't appear to notice Edgar, even though he was panting heavily. She was drawing on the wall in crayon. He was also fairly certain he heard her say, "Gaga, goo-goo."

Edgar crept into the room, and one of his hind legs got caught on a pool-cleaning pole. He had no hands to catch it with, and so it clanged to the ground. It sounded like a gunshot. The baby's body jerked. She spun around and shot Edgar a confused look. Her face and the front of her baby doll dress were covered in finger paint. It looked like a rainbow had melted on her.

Somehow, despite her considerably regressed age, her face was still completely recognizable.

"Oh, whoa. Holy shit. B-Beth?"

Beth's mouth opened in a perfect "O," and she squealed in a pitch so high that Edgar was not sure anyone else but him could hear it. She hit a lower pitch and then screamed, "Edgar! Edgar is doggie now! Yay!" She crawled toward him, maddeningly fast.

Edgar jumped and attempted to flee the scene, but his face collided with the nearest wall. He tried to get his bearings, but the dizziness won. Beth's tiny toddler arms formed a tight python grip around him.

"Eeeeee! I love'm doggies! I miss my Edgar baby!"

Edgar could barely breathe. He felt kisses all over his body, but they didn't feel like the kisses Beth dished out in the past, not even the super sloppy ones after a weekend bender in Mexico. It felt wrong, as many taboo forms of roleplay do a few moments after the seed has dried. But this was no fantasy. This was dog and baby, this was real life, and neither of them knew what the hell they wanted anymore.

"Well jerk me off, Jesus." Jack entered the guesthouse. Beth did not release her grip on Edgar. She looked up at Jack in stupid glee and screamed, "Hi, Jack-ee boy! Pick me up now!" Jack raised his eyebrow. He looked like he wanted to laugh, as if maintaining a sense of humor in this moment was the only thing that would keep him sane.

Edgar whimpered and gave Jack his best pitiful puppy dog face. "Help? Please?"

"I don't know. This is like some sort of poetic justice, isn't it?"

"Aw, come on, man."

Jack closed his eyes, leaned back against the wall, and pressed both of his palms against his forehead. "What did I do to deserve this?"

CHAPTER THIRTEEN

MAHBOOB STROKED HIS thick, dark eyebrows like favored pets. He locked the front door to Cosmo's Custom Costumes, double-checked it with a tug, silenced the jangle of the welcoming bell, flipped the Open sign to Closed, and flicked off the lights in the front room. The day was done almost as soon as it had begun. The first of November was always the busiest day of the year at Cosmo's. Rental returns. Discounts on year-old makeup and spirit gum. Pre-orders for the coming year of costume parties and other dress-up nonsense. They made a point of only being open for a few short hours in the morning, knowing full well the majority of their customers would still be in bed. This tactic considerably increased the amount of late fees they were able to charge.

It was a living. The family got by. They were able to pay rent, to eat. Not much more beyond that.

Mahboob wanted more for himself, for his family. Even though he felt resentment toward his mother and younger brother in many ways, they all worked hard. They deserved something better. Why hadn't they received their piece of the pie yet?

He strutted past the counter, stopping briefly to make sure he removed the tray from the register, even though he was certain he had because he counted the money twice just moments ago and placed it in the office safe. He moved toward the back of the shop, a trek that always felt like hours.

At the end of the dimly lit hall, Cosmo greeted him at the entrance to the back room. He leaned against the doorjamb, looking relaxed, as if he had not a care in the world. Cosmo was everything Mahboob was not. The spitting image of their late father. Skin like butterscotch pudding. Clean-shaven, unblemished face and a body chiseled by Michelangelo. Thick, dark hair slicked back like Lugosi in his finest moments, though this 'do was everyday wear, not just for the Halloween season. Women were always at his beck and call. It was sickening how perfect he was.

Cosmo was also Maa's favorite and had been ever since he was born one year after Mahboob. He knew it, Mahboob knew it, the whole world knew it. But nobody said it. Probably because they didn't have to. Mothers of multiple children would never publicly admit it, but deep in their hearts they definitely chose favorites.

"Come, bhaiya," Cosmo said, beckoning Mahboob with both of his log-sized arms, a faux-jovial smile pasted to his face. "The shishyas awaiting our judgment time. Maa is awaiting."

Mahboob shuddered at the sound of the word "Maa." Cosmo had always been the golden boy, with Mahboob relegated to toady status. Everything Mahboob did was wrong, even when it was unequivocally right. If he did something wrong on purpose, it was twice as wrong. He just couldn't win. But he loved Maa, respected her, and so he followed his brother.

Cosmo slung his arm around Mahboob's shoulder as they walked. Mahboob couldn't show weakness, even though the left side of his body felt like it was going to collapse. He couldn't let his brother win.

They entered the back room, lit only by candlelight at Maa's request. At her advanced age, she couldn't handle fluorescent lighting for more than a few moments and would only leave the comfort of the store after dusk, and even then protected by a thick black shroud so no one could see what she looked like. Mahboob couldn't recall the last time he had even seen her face. Truth be told, he didn't miss it much. Some people have a face only a mother could love, but when that face belongs to the mother herself, it's a difficult concept for anyone to wrap their mind around.

The shishyas sat in a semi-circle on the chilled concrete floor, looking as if they were awaiting a sacrifice to begin. Mahboob didn't know any of their real names. He only knew them as the Furry Five: Black Bunny, Blue Fox, Pink Kitty, Purple Lion, and Yellow Cub. They were not wearing their costumes now, because that would have been silly, but Mahboob knew who was who because he had created their costumes, meticulously tailored them and custom fit them to each young man (and young woman in the case of Pink Kitty). He received no praise, no accolades, but none of that mattered because Mahboob took pride in his work. The quality of the craft was of the utmost importance. Self-satisfaction got him through the day.

The codenames for each of the Furry Five were their real names as far as Mahboob was concerned. He couldn't be bothered to learn anything beyond that. Only two would graduate this course, even if all five succeeded at their tasks, though history had shown that result would have been as likely as a dog cleaning up its own feces in the yard. This being the most difficult test meant someone would fail. Someone would be punished.

A few candles decorated the room, some on the floor, two placed in steel sconces on the wall. In the far corner sat Maa. She was enveloped in darkness, sitting in a replica of a throne atop a concrete platform. Neither Maa nor the throne were clearly visible. Only a nocturnal animal would have been able to make out her complete shape. The only parts of her the candlelight illuminated were her legs—varicose veins, overgrown peach fuzz, and loose pink skin. If Maa knew her legs were visible, she would likely slit the throat of whoever was near her. Since Cosmo was currently in the closest proximity, sitting just below her in a folding chair, Mahboob said nothing.

"Sit, Mahboob, my sweet," she said, her voice thick with phlegm. Her gnarled, clawed hand reached out and gently stroked Cosmo's greasy hair. Mahboob was shocked her flesh did not burn from exposure to the slight light. "We are about to grade the final exams."

Inside, Mahboob frowned because Maa stated the obvious. She had always thought him the dunce, but in truth his brain was worth three of Cosmo. He was the genius, the artist, and the shitworker trapped in a single body. Why couldn't she see that?

Outside, he grinned, his coffee-stained, plaque-ridden teeth barely exposed in the darkness.

Mahboob sat in a second folding chair just below Maa's throne.

He could smell Maa's body odor. Like a mix of patchouli and day-old trout. No matter how many years he had smelled her, it never magically became prettier.

"Purple Lion," Cosmo said, already hamming it up. He loved the limelight, especially when it was not his to hog. "You are the first."

The young man Mahboob only knew as Purple Lion stood. He was short, thin, unassuming. A basic mop of dirty hair. He could have been a neighbor, a busboy, a newsstand clerk, a choirboy, a scientist. The perfect assassin.

"Everything went as planned," Purple Lion said, his confidence oozing from his lips. He looked down at his hand, apparently examining his fingernails in the candlelight. Mahboob hated his smug expression, or what he could see of it in the dim light.

"Eh?" Maa said. "Speak up. The tongue has its own volume knob, you know . . . "

Purple Lion raised his voice a few decibels. "Everything went as planned. Naturally. A house party in Silver Lake. I hid in the coat closet until I was certain everything worked and the partygoers were sleeping like little babies. Then I waited in the coffee shop across the street, watched as the first of them left the house. The transformation was a success."

"Good, good," Maa rasped in the background, more to herself than to Purple Lion or anyone else in the room.

"You may sit," Cosmo said. "Black Bunny. You are now standing up to tell."

Black Bunny was a chubby boy. He looked like someone saying "Boo" to his face might terrify him. Mahboob could tell he was reluctant to stand but did so anyway. He had nothing to say and everything to say at once. Mahboob had known from day one of this year's ritual that this weakling wouldn't make the cut, and it appeared his instincts were correct. Only a skilled shishya could accomplish what they needed. This, Black Bunny was not.

"Well?" Cosmo said. "Keep us out of suspense. Speaking to us your work now. There is not all day to wait for you."

"The potion . . . " Black Bunny began. "The potion . . . it didn't . . . activate. I don't know what went wrong. It should have been fine. I think someone must have done something to my—"

"Automatic disqualification," Cosmo said. "Failure with capital 'F.' Please be leaving and not come back."

"B-but—"

"Go! Or Maa be choosing to turn you into earthworm like you are!"

Mahboob rolled his eyes at the overly dramatic display. His brother got some sick satisfaction out of intimidating the weak.

Black Bunny started to skitter out of the room, but he halted at the sound of Maa shrieking, "Stop!" Her voice made nails on a chalkboard sound like a soothing lullaby.

"Come to me," Maa said, beckoning to him with one red claw, "and perhaps you will be forgiven. Perhaps."

Black Bunny paused for a moment, then shuffled toward her, his jelly rolls jiggling beneath his shirt. He stood in front of Mahboob and Cosmo, just a few feet from Maa's throne. Mahboob gripped his seat. He wondered if Black Bunny had any idea what came next. He didn't care much for the boy, but he didn't wish the ill fate that surely awaited him. Banishment would have been more than suitable. But he was not the one in charge.

"Closer," Maa said, her voice a husky whisper. Black Bunny obeyed the command as if he had no choice in the matter. He was mesmerized. Maa stroked the nape of his neck, and for a split second her flesh looked like it had taken a dip in the fountain of youth. Not a wrinkle, a blemish, nor a wart.

But the illusion only lasted long enough to make Black Bunny relax.

Black Bunny stuttered. "I'm . . . uh . . . I . . . " Before he had a chance to form a coherent thought, Maa's hand, now looking as grotesque as always, lashed out at his throat, her fingernail slashing the pudgy flesh. It was a clean and straight cut, as if sliced with the sharp edge of a ruler. Blood spurted from the wound. Black Bunny gasped for air. He couldn't scream or beg, and even the largest Band-Aid in the world wouldn't have saved him now. The carotid was severed.

Maa pulled him closer to her. A long, thin, deep red forked tongue lashed out from the darkness with animalistic precision. It lapped at Black Bunny's throat, catching as much precious gushing blood as it could. Very little made it to the floor. When finally sated,

Maa released Black Bunny from her grip. His body thumped to the floor and went into a brief seizure before going still.

The room was silent, but not for long. There was no shock to be had. Death was expected in this group, encouraged even. The shishyas knew what they had signed up for. It was what they thrived on. The chaos of life brought to a screeching halt for no apparent reason. Onward to the next life. Samsara forever.

"Praise Kali," Cosmo said.

"Praise Kali," Mahboob said, his voice closer to a whisper.

"Mahboob," Maa said. "You will take care of this later, yes?"

Mahboob cursed his mother in his mind, the only part of him she had zero control over. "Yes, Maa."

"Pink Kitty, darling," Cosmo said, leering at her as if he had never seen a female before. Mahboob didn't see the big deal, but he knew Cosmo would fawn over an eggplant if it had been graced with a vagina. Pink Kitty's breasts may have been perfectly crafted pillows, but her chipmunk cheeks looked like bees had stung her one too many times. Still, her mind was more attractive than most females Mahboob had encountered, and her devotion to the dakini, to Maa, was impressive. That counted for something. "Do telling us your tale. We are in the waiting."

Pink Kitty looked proud. "My group was small," she said, "Only a dozen or so. But *very* special."

"Oh?" Cosmo leaned closer to Pink Kitty. His blatant flirtation sickened Mahboob. He wanted to induce vomiting.

Pink Kitty paused, presumably for dramatic effect. "I was able to bribe myself into a private party for Kirk Dietrich."

"The actor?" Mahboob asked. The game had changed drastically. His poker face vanished and was replaced with shock and awe.

"One and the same."

"But," Mahboob said. "But I not recall this star coming into the store. I would remember such an instance. When this happening?"

"Dietrich didn't come into the store," Pink Kitty said. "His assistant did. I arranged the whole thing. Been working as an intern at Paramount since summertime, bringing coffee to the people who bring coffee to the more important people. As for the actual bribe, well . . . I'll keep those details private if it's all the same to you." She winked. Mahboob got the message.

"And the costume for this . . . this Kirk Dietrich person?" Cosmo asked. It sickened Mahboob even further that his brother had never even heard of the great actor from such classic films as *Gunpowder & Cigarettes*, *The Sorcerer's Tomb*, and *Bitchin' Summer*. A real man's man. An Eastwood, a Wayne for the modern generation, but with a distinct Everyman vibe. Cosmo had no sense of culture. Art was a foreign concept to him, as foreign as their family was to this country.

"Penis Head."

Mahboob gasped at this realization. He couldn't withhold his joy. He remembered every moment of creating this costume, snickering with the glee of a teenage boy who had just seen his first glimpse of bush on a TV. He had wondered who would wear it and become its unsuspecting victim. He had no idea it would go to someone so famous, so dashing. A lover of lovers. Though he felt slightly conflicted that it had ruined one of his favorite actors, it was his true claim to fame. He allowed himself the pride he so dearly deserved.

Maa hissed from the darkness. "Yes. You understand our cause, shishya. The perfect choice. Punish the rich, the pale. The whores of Hollywood. While we struggle, they continue to thrive. To them, we have always been faceless. They will soon know who we are. And they will not forget us."

Cosmo offered Pink Kitty a golf clap. "Bravo, bravo. But final judgment yet to be over. Yellow Cub next."

Yellow Cub was almost in tears. His long dark hair and sparkling eyes made him look almost feminine. "Everything was going so well. I swear . . . but everyone at the party I went to . . . they . . . they melted."

"Whaaaa?" Cosmo's nose wrinkled.

"Melted into puddles of mush. Within seconds. I couldn't stop it. I guess it's 'cause I tried to get creative, but it didn't . . . it all—"

"What you mixing potion with?"

"I sprinkled it onto the chocolate cupcakes they were serving. Man . . . I don't know . . . "

"Fool! Not remembering rule number 33: No mixing the potion with dairy."

"What? What the hell are you talking about? I never saw these rules."

"Was designed for activation only with alcohol. Useless idiot!"

"No. Wait. I—"

"It no matters. You know what you must do. This is not just failure, but misobedience of rules! You must pay!" Yellow Cub was sobbing now. Mahboob felt embarrassed for him. And he knew the punishment would be far too harsh. It always was when Maa was the one dishing it out, when Cosmo was her avid cheerleader.

Yellow Cub took hesitant steps toward Maa's throne. He was contractually obligated to accept his fate, but this didn't make the task any easier. He entered Maa's warm embrace. The darkness seemed to swallow him. Even though Mahboob was inches away from Yellow Cub, could have twisted his nipple if he so desired, he could no longer see his face.

"There, there," Maa said. "It will be alright. I promise."

A squelching sound came from the darkness, followed by a scream so loud it almost drowned out the subsequent tearing and slurping noises. Mahboob wiggled his finger in his ear to rid himself of his temporary deafness.

Yellow Cub stumbled out of the darkness, the top of his head cleanly scalped. His brain was exposed, almost resembling a wrinkled fetus. He howled as he ran from the room, likely from sheer muscle memory, and only got a few feet away before he collapsed to the floor in the hallway. Maa hummed in the background, and Mahboob knew she was strong again. She was finally full.

For now.

"Mahoob," Maa said.

"Yes, Maa. I know."

"Ah," Cosmo said, "last one, yes? Blue Fox?"

Blue Fox stroked his long, wild goatee. His head was bald by choice, not by nature. His eyes were the size and color of chia seeds. The circles around them were even darker, as if someone had tricked him with a black eye telescope. His lips were pressed tightly together.

He simply smiled. He knew he had won. Mahboob was sure of it. The smug confidence in the man's tiny eyes proved there was no contest.

CHAPTER FOURTEEN

JACK DIDN'T EVEN bother to turn his head when he grinned at Kat. He only used one side of his mouth. He only looked at her out of the corner of his eye. Kat could tell he was doing his best to comfort her, but she knew it was an act. Jack was no thespian. It was a kind gesture from the only male who had ever truly treated her with respect, but even Jack couldn't fake the fact that she was a disgusting beast now. Any hopes she'd had of becoming more than friends with Jack had been torn apart and shat upon this morning.

She slightly shifted in an attempt to subvert the faux affection, but there was only an inch or two to move before she was pressed up against the inside of the car door. She felt a tear near her hip, then slid her hand to her side and felt something sticky. Jack didn't notice. His eyes were focused on the road now. He wasn't going to be happy about whatever goo she'd left on his seat. She'd have to clean it up later, when he wasn't around. When all of this was over.

Beth and Edgar were both napping in the back seat. Under other circumstances, it might have been sweet. Instead, it was just beautiful, temporary respite.

"Okay," Jack said, "so we can't carry Beth around with us. She's too much of a burden."

"We're just going to leave a toddler alone?"

"No . . . well, no. I mean . . . it's just Beth. Remember after graduation when Edgar left her passed out in the car after she took too many ludes? It's not like it's going to be any different than that, really."

"If you say so."

"She'll be fine. Let's just drop her off at my place, get her settled, then I'm taking you—"

"No doctors."

"I was just gonna say I can take you home so can rest for a bit. Or you can come with Edgar and me to see Wade. Your call."

"K," Kat said.

"Which is it?"

"Take me with you. Please. I don't want to be alone." Even speaking was becoming a challenge for Kat. It was as if the costume was absorbing into her bloodstream now, affecting all of her senses and her faculties. Rotting her from the outside in. She realized this was probably what dying felt like, because this was likely what dying actually *was*. There was nothing Jack could do to truly protect her. Unless they somehow successfully managed to get to the source of this problem and figure out how to reverse it, she wouldn't last more than another day, perhaps two if she turned her moxie up to eleven.

She couldn't stop thinking about what Hannah had said to her just before they left her house.

That's boy's so good to you.

It was something Kat already knew. She wasn't a complete idiot, but it had taken her best friend vocalizing it for her to realize the weight of the statement. Never had it been more true than today. Jack had been there for her every step of the way, despite the fact that she looked like a Garbage Pail Kid come to life. Hazmat Kat.

"So I just remembered something," Jack said. "Something I read a few years back. Must have been in some science magazine, I guess." Jack was always reading. If he didn't have his nose in a book or periodical at least twice a day, he was likely to go into severe withdrawal. Kat liked to tease him and call him a knowledge junkie, but deep down she was impressed by the fact that he was so absorbed with words, that he found strength in learning. He'd somehow managed without his addiction so far today, but it was probably tearing him up inside.

"Oh, yeah? What's that?"

"Apparently it's possible for armadillos to transmit leprosy to humans. Crazy, right?"

Kat scrunched up her face in confusion. Her left cheek drooped, her right cheek tensed up. "Okay. And?"

"Well, yeah, that's just it. And? Maybe it means something, but what?"

Kat did not respond.

"I don't know," Jack continued. "I just thought maybe . . . fuck, I'm an asshole. That's so goddamned insensitive. I mean, that's the last thing you want to—"

"Jack. No. Whatever this is that's happening to me, I don't think you're going to find the answer in an article."

"That's exactly why we need to get you to a doctor."

Kat turned and stared at Jack. "Jesus, can we please fucking drop the doctor shit already?" Invisible fire screamed from her eyes, burned through his skull.

"We can put off going to Cosmo's until tomorrow. Or I'll get everyone together and we'll go tonight without you. This is more important. You need to—"

"No!" Kat meant business. Jack shrunk away, defeated.

"Hey, what the hell is going on up there?" Edgar's voice was hoarse, groggy.

Beth cried uncontrollably.

"Dammit," Jack said.

Kat was grateful for the fact she would likely never live long enough to be a housewife.

———◆———

In the sunlight, the young man standing outside the back door almost looked like a familiar version of a friend Hannah once knew. A friend who had since passed away, whose obituary showed up hidden in the classified ads, somewhere between someone selling a Super Nintendo sans games and a Help Wanted ad for a male Hot Dog on a Stick cashier.

But then the clouds obscured the sun, and she wondered how this brute of a man could have ever been the person she thought he was. Not now, not ever.

Hannah wasn't sure how, but somehow she knew this man was Lucas, but also knew it wasn't him anymore. Far from it. It didn't look a thing like him. It just *felt* like him.

It was the costume that clued her in. Jumpsuit, work boots, bowler's cap. She had only briefly said hello to Lucas last night, but this was definitely what he was wearing. Some crap character from some crap movie, the name of which she couldn't recall for the life of her.

He had changed, no . . . *been* changed like so many of her once-normal friends. He was larger, dangerously attractive despite his poor choice in wardrobe. But in those other friends, even though there had been a dramatic physical change, there still remained some semblance of soul. She did not think this was the case with this hulked-out version of Lucas. He'd always been an asshole, but on rare occasions he was uncharacteristically kind. Now, however, the likelihood of him having a friendly bone in his body was slim to nil. She started with a flirty wave to build rapport, to see if her intuition was off, if the maniacal look in his eyes would melt into warmth, but they were no longer human eyes.

They were feral. Hungry.

"L-Lucas? Is that you? Are you okay?"

"Nope and nope. Allow me to introduce you to Grady Sullivan."

She backed away from the edge of the pool, swam to the middle, the splashing of her tail the only sound save some doves cooing from inside a nearby hedge. She hoped this new Lucas—this *Grady*—either couldn't swim or would decide he didn't feel like getting wet on this cool November morning. Later it would be much warmer. Later he would definitely feel like taking a dip.

But Hannah didn't think "later" was on the agenda. And she was short on options.

Grady approached the pool with a gait straight out of serial killer school. Stiff and determined. A walk you could run and temporarily hide from, but never truly escape. But it was not a practiced stroll. It was natural, as if he had been walking this way his whole life and no one had noticed until now.

Hannah screamed for Jonah, then screamed again, louder, then decided to save her breath because she remembered Jonah was deep in the corridors of her house, in the second guest bathroom, likely giving birth to a big beautiful brown baby. Again. And Jonah, he had this peculiar habit of listening to his headphones loudly whenever he went #2, like he was ashamed to listen to his own flatulence.

Instead of being here to save her from something potentially very, very bad, he was probably blasting some of that atonal sensitive man-rock Hannah loathed.

She wanted to speak to Lucas, find him somewhere deep inside this Grady shell, reason with his possible insanity. Only to buy a little more time, just some time to find the receipt to her fate and make a preferential return.

He was almost at the edge of the pool now. He cracked his knuckles, a smile, and a joke. "Sorry, Charlie," he said. His voice was unexpectedly raspy, as if he had been yelling for hours and hadn't allowed his throat time to heal. "This little chicken of the sea's about to get sliced, diced, and fricasseed." Hannah wrinkled her nose at the bad one-liner. If she weren't so damned terrified, she would have snapped back at him.

Lining the yard near the pool, in a perfectly formed "L," were rows of large polished stones the size of mangoes. Grady quickly squatted and picked one up. Before Hannah had the sense to dive down deep, Grady hurled the stone with a pitcher's precision. One take. It struck Hannah in the temple.

The world went black.

———◆———

When Hannah awoke from her stupor, the first thing she expected to see was Jonah hovering over her, kissing her forehead and telling her he was so, so sorry and everything was going to be just fine because the ambulance and the authorities were on their way. And yes, of course it was all only a dream. The fish tail would be gone, her bathing suit bottom would be hugged tight against her. Life would continue as normal.

But when didn't Jonah appear before her, she absently wondered how long it could take a young man to defecate, how many back issues of *Esquire* or *Maxim* could he possibly have been reading in there, so far away at the other end of the property. To some young men, the latrine was a library.

And she knew for certain what she was experiencing was no dream.

She felt numbness on her arms—or rather *didn't* feel it, and it took a few seconds for her to realize she was lying supine on the ground a few feet from the pool. She was tied tightly around her upper arms and her midsection. Rope. She had no idea why there would even be rope at her house. Her parents had no use for rope. It probably belonged to the help.

A gag clogged her mouth. It tasted like fresh laundry. She felt a faint throbbing down below, where her beautiful legs once were. She was dizzy and weak. Something sizzled nearby on the grill. A familiar scent wafted into her nose, and she realized she was beyond starved. Jonah was supposed to bring her a sandwich. She really wanted a sandwich.

Suddenly Grady hovered over her, startling her from her hungry thoughts. He held a plate from her mother's favorite china collection, and Hannah briefly thought, *Wait, he had time to tie me up* and *go digging around in the china hutch? Seriously . . . where the hell is Jonah?*

Grady dug into some indeterminate piece of meat on his plate and shoved a slice in his mouth. He chewed it slowly and loudly, his lips smacking like a child trying to annoy his parents. Hannah mumbled through her gag.

"Sorry to silence those pretty lil' lips of yours," he said, "but you have one hell of a loud fucking mouth. Anyone ever tell you that? You just never know when to shut up."

Hannah looked up at Grady's plate. He seemed to notice her desperation and said, "Oh, I don't think you want any of what I'm having. Just trust me on that. Might be an eensy bit awkward." He took another large bite and continued talking with his mouth full, juice dripping down his chin. "There sure is plenty to go around, though. I was thinking of inviting the neighbors, but then I'd have to kill them, too, and that would be just plain Snoresville. Plus . . . I'm having way too much goddamned fun with you all to myself."

The pain below Hannah's waist intensified. Her torso tensed up. She attempted to scream behind the gag, but only a muffled grunt came out. Her mind finally started adjusting to reality, but it was still weak and hazy. She had a sinking sensation that she needed to get back in the water so her scales wouldn't dry out. She hummed through her gag again, tried to cry out. Tried to enunciate Jonah's name.

"Screw it. You wanna see what I've been up to? Of course you do. Might as well. You don't have a choice anyway. I've never been good

at keeping secrets for very long. One of my many character flaws."
Grady lowered himself to the ground and crouched, then lifted
Hannah's head into his lap and cradled it. He rubbed her hair gently,
forced her head higher, and pointed it in the direction of her tail.

Or what had once been her tail.

What had once been her legs.

Half of Hannah's gorgeous shimmering green mermaid tail had
been removed vertically, sliced from caudal fin nearly to her waist.
An enormous puddle of thick, dark blood glistened where the
missing half had once been. The other half twitched miserably. The
blood stained the concrete, which was going to piss her mother off
so much, but Hannah couldn't really worry about that because she
was still bleeding and omigod she was dying and would definitely
be full-blown dead if Jonah didn't come save her and get her to a
hospital before she lost too much blood. If it wasn't already too late.
If her fate hadn't already been sealed. She screamed and cried again,
but she knew deep down her attempts to save herself were futile.
Jonah was probably dead, his throat slit, a handsome corpse sitting
upon the toilet. He wasn't coming to save her.

And she would never see Kat again, never have another chance
to share space with her best friend in the world. That perhaps hurt
worse than anything else she was feeling at the moment, physically
or emotionally.

"Funny thing about this," Grady continued, "I've always
wondered what it'd be like to eat your pussy. And now I guess I kinda
know, huh? My compliments to the chef! Oh, wait . . . that's me! Tee-
hee!" He laughed maniacally, like an overacted version of a cartoon
super villain. He was loving every second of it.

Hannah's eyes were drowning in tears. She wanted to vomit. Her
head felt like it was floating. She thought of rainbows and pacifiers
and Sour Patch Kids and bunny tails and FroYo, anything to blind
the pain with false pleasure. So much blood had left her body . . .
how could she have lost so much blood and still be alive?

It was an appropriate thought to ponder as darkness blanketed
her, as death wormed its way into her heart.

———— ◆ ————

Jonah hobbled out into the backyard, his legs and rump still sore
from sitting on the toilet for too long. He had always taken his time,

ever since he was a toddler in potty training mode. He enjoyed a good shit, and to be honest he felt it was his right as a man to appreciate the simple pleasures in life. Some habits were non-negotiable.

But his bowel movements had been problematic all morning. He wasn't enjoying his bathroom time today in the slightest. And, as much as he'd attempted to deny it, he knew why.

He'd been shitting out Ken. The human body likely didn't agree well with cannibalism on its first attempt, especially when that attempt was involuntary.

He tried to keep his breathing steady. None of it made sense. It couldn't be true. Not a chance. It was just a bad batch of drugs, making him see things that weren't there, feel sensations that weren't real. It was just a hot dog he'd eaten. Not his friend. A simple fucking hot dog. One well past its due date, but not one made of man. He'd had some bad chorizo in Tijuana once, and Montezuma's revenge had hit him hard. Almost pure liquid for days. It had been the worst weekend of his life.

But it was nothing like what he was experiencing now.

He munched on a cheese sandwich, hoped to God it wasn't one of his good friends. Unlikely, but he couldn't help but wonder if he'd think that about every meal for the rest of his life. At this point, it probably didn't matter. He'd already stepped over the edge. He could never claim to not be a cannibal. Once human flesh slid down a person's gullet, there was no turning back. Life would never be the same. Even switching to a plant-based diet from this day forward wouldn't absolve him.

It was his second sandwich, for which he felt eternally guilty, but the first one was just so damned good. He would pay for those carbs later. Big time. He would have to make sure to wake up early tomorrow so he could spend an extra hour in the gym, focus on fitness.

If he could stay off the toilet for longer than half an hour, that is.

He thought he saw Hannah sunbathing by the pool, but wondered why she was doing so on the ground instead of a chair. He felt immense guilt again because she probably could have used a hand getting out of the water. He was already trying to form the perfect apology, hoping the words would come to him before he reached her.

The sun temporarily blinded him as he spoke. He used his hand as a visor. "Hey, sorry babe. This was the last of your bread. I'm a dick. You can have half if you want, or I can just go pick you up someth—"

He stopped. Dropped the sandwich. The plate shattered on the concrete. Tiny shards of porcelain bounced into the pool.

"Hannah!"

He ran to his girlfriend, if she could have ever been referred to as such. He ran to the only girl he had ever wanted to spend time with while fully clothed, even though he had rarely worn a shirt in her presence. She was the only female he had ever opened up to about being the fat kid who was bullied all through elementary school, about how his confidence was nonexistent before he discovered the wonders of CrossFit.

He struggled with the knots around her body. After a few moments he was finally able to remove the ropes. He ripped the gag from her mouth, tried to avoid looking at the carnage below her waist, but his left eye kept wandering. So much blood, more than he ever thought could be trapped in such a tiny, beautiful body. The mess smelled like a mix of ocean, copper, and feces. Jonah breathed through his mouth. He then realized he should attempt CPR. And he did. Sloppily. It did nothing. He knew it was only a formality.

He looked up to the stone bar and saw something strikingly familiar sitting on one of the stools. Something that hadn't been there before he wandered off to the restroom.

A bowler's cap.

Jonah had seen this before. Recently. But he couldn't quite place it. It was only a matter of time. It wasn't just a clue. It was the next step to the truth.

He pulled Hannah's body close to his, hoping her eyes would shift, that her lips would part and she would get to release some final words, that he would have the honor of sharing a tear-jerking Hollywood moment up here in the Hollywood Hills with her. But there was nothing present in this sad scene but cold, rank death.

And the bitter taste of vengeance.

CHAPTER FIFTEEN

I N SOME WAYS, Lucas Lane didn't strongly adhere to the values commonly associated with WASPs. Yes, he was a proud member of the Republican Party, but he wasn't a pro-lifer, wasn't even close to a bible thumper, though he had begrudgingly attended Sunday school as a young boy. Despite these transgressions, and despite his transformation, there was something a little off in his mind about killing a baby. His moral dilemma was further greyed by the fact that the baby was technically just shy of legal drinking age.

However, despite his misgivings, he still went through with the act. Grady didn't mind at all, and Lucas was now committed to his character.

He'd never liked Beth, always felt she was a bitch who took pride in her bitchery. Any outsiders would have been perturbed by the brief relationship he and Beth had, wondering why he had even chosen to date her. These would be the same people who were blissfully unaware that young men who relied too much on their smaller heads tended to put up with a great deal of punishment if it meant there was an orgasm waiting at the end of the whip. It was one of the few things Lucas and Grady had immediately agreed upon when their minds had merged.

Lucas didn't believe all women were evil. Far from it. He believed his mother to be a saint among saints. She had raised him and Carey without any help from their dear old Dad who quit the family for a girl who might or might not have still been in high school. The resulting alimony checks contained many zeros, which kept them well. His mother was still living large in the Hills, and Lucas and Carey were each living on their own, thanks to a few of those zeros.

But that was a sentiment from another life. Did that mean Lucas might harm his mother now? It was difficult to say. Grady was currently steering the ship, and Lucas's former eyes were shut, sewn over, forgotten, a memory of a made-up dream.

He had far bigger problems to worry about at the moment. The most significant: trying to figure out how to do something artistic with Beth's insides. It wasn't as easy as it looked in the movies.

Earlier he'd been stalking around Hannah Harper's house, hoping for some sort of clue that would make sense out of his present situation. But what he'd found there made life even more interesting.

Hannah by the pool, going through a second puberty just like him. And she had some visitors as well. Edgar Cotton, now a stinking dog. Kat Dyer, a walking bag of putrid flesh. Yet Jack Lantin looked his normal self, as did Hannah's latest fuck whose name Lucas could not recall. He couldn't figure out why some of them had changed while others hadn't, but eventually his patient eavesdropping paid off. They'd brought up the possibility that the costume shop was the source of all their troubles, and it all made sense. Lucas felt like a simpleton for not coming up with the idea himself.

And then there was Beth. When Jack brought her out, uncomfortably cradling her in his arms, Hannah acted as if she didn't even know Beth was on the premises. But there she was, in all her infantile glory.

Jack, Kat, and Edgar took Beth with them, presumably for safe keeping. He knew he'd track them down later. There were only so many places they could go and feel comfortable enough to let their guard down. And he had business to attend to at Hannah's house first.

But once Grady had finished with Hannah, once he had sated both his appetite and the ache in his skull, he headed out to find the rest of them.

Stalking wasn't all it was cracked up to be. As any cop who had been on a stakeout would claim, it involves about 75 percent waiting and 25 percent trying to forget you're waiting. But Grady was determined. And his instincts were spot on. He'd guessed correctly that they'd head to Jack and Edgar's apartment. He should have been born a bloodhound.

The waiting hadn't been much of an issue. Not long after he arrived, Jack, Edgar, and Kat left Beth alone in one of the bedrooms. They were gathering in the living room, likely discussing their next steps.

They even left the bedroom window open. It was broad daylight, so what did they have to worry about?

Grady decided to make his move. He was an opportunist, and what a great opportunity this was that had fallen right into his lap. They had no reason to suspect Beth would be in any danger. No one was following them. No one knew where they were. So they thought. Stupid to be so careless, but Grady would cut them some slack.

This time.

Soon enough, they'd know better than to let their guard down so easily.

He had to silence Beth immediately. A quick whack to the back of her head and she was out before she even knew she needed to make a peep. Looking down at her tiny, frail new body, he decided the baby thing didn't bother him all that much, certainly not if it was going to get in the way of him having some good old-fashioned fun. It was important to prioritize. Today he fancied himself a decorator, and the decorations he needed for this special occasion were sealed up tight inside a toddler's body. He merely needed to open it up, dig in, and begin creating his masterpiece.

It ended up not being worth the effort. She wasn't able to fight back, wouldn't have even if she were conscious, which made it difficult to enjoy. He yearned for the moment before the knife slid in the belly like a finger into slightly melted butter, the moment where he'd look in her eyes and she knew her life was about to roll its credits. But killing an unconscious baby, even if it wasn't truly a baby, just did absolutely nothing for him. Pointless, really. He wanted someone who knew what their life was worth and how terrified they were of losing it. Someone who yearned to grow old but realized it would never happen.

He'd had a taste of it earlier with Hannah, and now he wanted more. Power was a potent drug, and nothing offered a greater high than playing God.

He already knew where his next stop would be after he was done with Beth. His next visit would be even more personal.

Grady was beginning to grow bored with what was left of Beth. His mojo just wasn't flowing. And there was so little he could do with a fresh corpse that hadn't already been done before, especially one so small. He tried to make the scene look shocking, write something unique, elegant, and cryptic on the wall in her blood, but the result was just a trite cliché, so he smeared the horrible haiku away. Hannibal Lecter, he was not. He felt more like a failed contestant on an interior design reality show, the guy who was about to be sent home despite thinking he had the challenge in the bag.

It was all in the editing. Some schmuck could think he was loveable during his stint on a show, then when the program aired he'd realize the producers had somehow manipulated him into a villain. It was a tactic Grady appreciated. The camera's eye told many lies. It was up to human hands to manipulate these fabrications as they saw fit.

In truth, Grady Sullivan had never been known for being the artistic type. Just a lean, mean, killing machine. Lucas decided to accept the new gifts he'd been given. There was no need to be ashamed. Some men were meant to be surgeons, some Nobel Prize winners. Some, bringers of death and destruction.

He had a few things to be proud of in his former life. He fancied himself a progressive psychopath with a strong moral center. He loved red pandas, even once donating $1,000 to a small endangered species charity in the Eastern Himalayas. And he'd do it all over again. Even now. He had enough money to do it as many times as he wanted. Perhaps they'd see a donation from Mr. Grady Sullivan soon. That would be a real hoot.

The creative cat wasn't clawing him anymore, and so he decided to quit and leave the room. Probably not a good idea to overstay his welcome. Someone would come to check on Beth soon enough.

After he squeezed through the window and hopped to the ground, he briefly considered taking a break, grabbing a quick bite to eat, but he couldn't decide if he wanted foie gras or chili fries. Decisions, decisions. Something told him that his old favorite restaurant *La Petite Vie* wouldn't allow Grady through their doors. A shame, really. They served such a wonderful spicy escargot skewer.

He recalled taking Beth there once, when he was Lucas, when he was still putting in the effort to take her on actual dates rather than just driving around Santa Monica with the windows rolled down, sharing a dime bag of snow. Beth hated *La Petite Vie*. Couldn't stop complaining about it for the rest of the night. Perhaps that had been the breaking point for him. He'd wanted to kill her on the spot, and it had been stewing in his mind ever since, but he didn't have the guts to go through with it until Grady was on his team. Better late than never.

He figured the rest of them would be glad to be rid of her, too. No one *really* liked Beth. They merely tolerated her because she happened to be a presence in their lives for so damned long. Good riddance to bad rubbish.

Just before he reached his vehicle, he heard something that made him absolutely giddy.

The sweet sound of screaming.

Timing was everything.

CHAPTER SIXTEEN

THERE'S SOMETHING ABOUT seeing a girl in the prime of her life disemboweled, her insides painted across a once-clean bedroom. It puts things into perspective. It solidifies the fact that young adulthood is just a tiny step on the road to rot. Some merely reach their destination earlier than others.

And Beth being trapped in an infant's body when she was ripped into pieces, had that made the situation worse? Kat wasn't sure if she was bothered by anything anymore. Just a few hours into her transformation, and the rot was already making her numb inside. To be honest, she welcomed the indifference. It was like Prozac, but more natural. Any other day and she might have taken a trip straight to the funny farm after seeing glistening entrails strewn across a bedroom. Today, not so much.

There was something else that disturbed Kat just as much as seeing the butchery in front of her, perhaps even more so. Edgar hadn't said a word after they had found what was left of Beth. This was the first time Kat had seen him silent for more than half a minute in all the years she had known him. He just sat hunched at the edge of the room, inches away from what appeared to be an ear. Not a peep, nor a whimper, nor an inappropriate wisecrack. It was a sure sign the end was nigh.

And now Hannah wasn't answering her phone. Six calls, straight to voicemail. Another apocalyptic event.

SEXY LEPER | 101

Every moment should have felt desperate now that the game had changed once again, but Kat didn't want anything to do with it. She was slowly but surely ceasing to care. Ceasing to be.

This slaughter was no coincidence. Someone was after them, but who? Jack said the obvious answer would have been someone from the costume shop, but Kat felt that just seemed like overkill. They'd already done their damage. What would they have to gain from killing them almost immediately? Didn't they at least want to see the fruits of their labor before harvesting?

No, this was something far more personal.

Jack was about to call the police, but Kat convinced him that would be an even worse decision than taking her to the doctor. Even if she and Edgar were able to go elsewhere to stay out of the public eye, Jack couldn't spend precious time being questioned. He'd be the primary suspect. A baby that wasn't even his found brutally murdered in his apartment? Hell, they'd lock him up and throw away the key. Good luck getting a fair trial.

Beth was gone. There was nothing they could do for her now. They would have to literally pick up the pieces later. They had to salvage what remained of their own lives first. If that was even possible.

They had to start building their army, however small it would be. They had to rally their troops and go to war.

———— ◆ ————

Wade Garrison's eyelids were puffy and deep red, the surrounding skin falling somewhere on the pink spectrum. He'd been committed to stoicism for so long he barely remembered what it was like to cry. It had been years, perhaps even dating back to his first loathsome moments outside of the womb, and his reunion with the emotion was bitter.

His body was slumped askew in his favorite tufted barrel chair, upholstered with mauve velvet, the front of its arms lined with brass nail heads. He clutched a partially crumpled photograph. He and Carey, at the top of the Eiffel Tower two years ago, taken by another tourist who also happened to be from Southern California. Carey when he was . . . Carey. Carey, who made a fake mustache with his finger. Carey, who wore a tank top that was far too small, even for his petite frame. Carey, who was supposed to be there for Wade forever.

And Wade, for Carey in return.

But waking up and seeing the love of his life transformed into a woman just did not compute. This was not the way things were supposed to work. It was the stuff of cruel, perverse nightmares. It wasn't like Carey had any desire to transition, and even if he had, he couldn't have done so overnight. No surgeon was that good, even the ones at the top of the pay scale. And no recovery was that quick. None of it made sense. There were dark forces at work in West Hollywood. Darker than usual.

The doorbell rang. He heard it, but also didn't hear it. He'd been crying so much he could feel his heartbeat throbbing within his skull. The sensation made the doorbell sound like a church bell that had been ringing for hours, but no one was coming to worship.

Then—a knock. Stern, solid. He almost reacted to that sound, but didn't care enough to bother.

A muffled voice shouted from the other side of the door. "Wade? Carey? You guys in there? Let me in. It's Jack."

Wade thought for a moment he might know someone named Jack, then realized he knew at least one person with every common male name. He probably knew five Johns (and two Jons), at least seven Mikes (one of whom spelled his name with a "y," and another who adamantly preferred to be called Michael), an uncountable amount of Joes and Steves, but perhaps only one Jack. Jack Lantin. Though, he also remembered Jack was often a nickname for John. So that could present a problem.

Wade figured the day couldn't get any worse, so he shuffled to the door while buttoning his shirt. He accidentally put the third button into the second hole, and everything fell apart from there. He left it. Fashionable perfection was the least of his worries today.

Jack knocked again. "Come on, guys. It's kind of an emergency."

"Be right there," he mumbled, with no regard to Jack's lack of superhuman hearing abilities. He glanced in the small mirror near the front door and discovered his bed head had somehow formed into a perfect fauxhawk. He winced at this tragedy, reached into a glass dish sitting on the entryway table, grabbed a blue butter mint, popped it into his mouth, smiled as it melted atop his tongue, and slipped it over to his cheek. It would have to do.

He opened the door. Jack's hair took up the majority of the

doorway. It looked like it had been molded by a hurricane masquerading as a hairstylist. "Hey, Wade. Jesus, you look like shit. You okay? Is Carey here? We really need to talk."

Wade bleated out a single-syllable laugh, and it seemed to startle Jack. Only for a moment.

"Can we come in?"

Wade shifted his body and allowed Jack to pass without a word. Jack grabbed a small handful of butter mints and threw them into his mouth. Wade tried his damnedest to avoid giving him the stink eye, but his damnedest wasn't good enough. "Got anything to drink? The harder the better. You're gonna need it when you hear what we have to tell you."

"Hmm. Bet I've got you beat. And who the hell is this 'we' you're talking about?" Wade tried to close the door behind Jack, but it stopped halfway. A girl in a hooded sweatshirt stood in the doorway, her hand held firmly against the door. Wade couldn't quite see her face hidden within the hood.

"Hey," she said quietly. Something looked wrong with her skin. It was raw, scaly, inflamed. Wade squinted and suddenly realized he knew who the poor soul buried under the horrible mess was.

"Kat . . . oh my God . . . what . . . "

"Just talk to Jack. Pour me a drink. I'm done talking."

Wade tried desperately to keep his jaw from becoming unhinged as Kat passed by him but was only moderately successful. He closed the door again. A quick moment after the latch clicked into the strike, there was a scratching at the door.

"Oh, what now?" When Wade opened the door, a black pug looked up at him with a stupid grin. Wade scrunched his nose. He loathed dogs. He didn't ever recall Jack having a pet. "Jack? Is this godforsaken thing yours? It can't be in here, you know. The shedding."

The dog shook its head and said, "Christ, Wade. Is this how you treat all your old friends?"

Wade blinked in slow motion, crushed his eyes tight, waited a few seconds, then opened them again. The dog was no longer there. *Thank God*, Wade thought. *Just a bad buzz. A talking dog. HA! Maybe it's time to sober up.*

"I'll take Peppermint Schnapps if you've got it," the dog said, now halfway to the kitchen. Wade spun around, spooked. He thought the voice sounded familiar, but he couldn't quite place it. "Or a White Russian. Whatever. Put it in a bowl. I don't care. The world fucking sucks and I just need to get hammered right now."

————— ◆ —————

Before Jack arrived at Wade's, he thought his story was going to blow his friend's mind. Hell, he still hadn't been able to adjust to it. However, he had to admit the tale of Carey's transformation was fairly impressive and somewhat nullified the impact of what he had to say, of what was already proven in the flesh due to Kat and Edgar being present, but he told his side anyway. He felt it was important to clarify before they took their next steps.

When Jack saw Carey in costume last night it had made him do a double take. He filed away a mental note to go ask the smoking hot babe for her number after he found Kat. Then he saw the hot girl link arms with Wade and kiss him. He did the math, shredded his mental note. He briefly wondered what Carey might look like naked in his new womanly body, then realized his thoughts were in bad form, thankfully before he had a chance to get an inappropriate chub. No guilt, only a passing and now deleted thought.

Jack explained what happened to Beth, glossing over how horrible the scene truly was. Partly for Edgar's sake, partly for his own. He was trying to forget what he'd seen. He knew he would never forget. It would haunt him in his worst nightmares for the rest of his life.

"My God," Wade said. He placed his fingers in pyramid formation, pressed them lightly to his lips, and stared down at the dining room table. "I'll be the first to admit I couldn't stand her, but even she didn't deserve *that*."

They sat silent for a moment, let Wade's statement sink in.

"One thing I think I still don't understand," Wade said. He pointed back and forth between Jack and himself. "Why not us? Why are we still normal?"

Jack explained their theory about the costume shop being behind this whole mess.

They all consumed more alcohol within a half hour than anyone should reasonably consider, though not enough to reach the point of incoherence. They had to make plans. Jack made sure to limit

Edgar's sips, much to Edgar's disappointment. But he was smaller now. His tolerance level had changed. At least he was starting to act relatively normal. Either the alcohol was doing a number on him or he was at least doing a wonderful job of pretending he wasn't thinking about Beth. Whatever it took to help him grieve.

Kat remained still, drinking away her sorrows in silence. Jack wanted to hold her, let her know he'd do everything in his power to help her, that he wouldn't let her down. But he couldn't make promises he wasn't certain he could keep. He also wasn't completely sure he should be touching her. Not so much for his own safety, but for fear she might turn to mush in his arms.

"I can't believe I made him leave," Wade said. "What was I thinking? I love him, Jack. I fucking love him, you know?"

"I know, man. Of course you do. You've been partners since the Cretaceous Period. Don't beat yourself up over it. We're all going through some weird shit right now."

"Uh, hey, guys," Edgar said, "I don't think either of you really deserve to say that. Hint, hint. Wink, wink."

Wade grunted. Jack shrugged. Edgar licked his front paws. Kat pulled her hoodie tighter over her head. What else could they do?

"Got any ghost, Wade? I need something to take the edge off."

"Sure. Yes. I think so."

"Just a bump would be cool."

Wade wandered off to find his stash. Jack looked at Kat again. She was his best friend, for lack of a more appropriate term. Their friendship was too special too be conveniently labeled. Always on the cusp of something romantic, yet never making the leap to anything further than friendship kisses. He cared for her in ways that were not easily classifiable, though traditionalists might beg to differ. He believed the aftermath of this Halloween tragedy would only bring them closer. It had to. But first they had to come out on the other side victorious. First they had to stop Kat from melting away into a pile of pus, blood, and crust.

Wade returned, shaking a small baggie in his hand. He quickly laid out a thin rail for himself, then dabbed a small pile onto Jack's pinky. They snorted simultaneously. Wade offered some to Kat, but she shook her head.

"We'll find Carey," Jack said. "But it'll have to wait. He can take of himself for now. Right now we need to put together a solid plan and head over to Cosmo's. Tonight. Tomorrow morning at the absolute latest."

"What do you think we should do?" Wade asked.

"Not sure yet. But that brings me to my next point. I need you to—"

Kat sobbed. Quietly. Jack could tell she was trying to hold her emotions in, but she wasn't succeeding. She caught him looking at her, then got up and ran toward the bathroom. He wanted to follow her, but this was probably one of those instances where she needed her space.

A few moments passed before anyone spoke. Jack could feel the liquor and the coke worming through his system, forming a solid bond and working for the greater good.

"Okay," Jack said. "So Wade . . . what I need you to do for me now is wait here in case Carey comes back." He paused for a few beats. "And watch Edgar for me."

As if it were previously scripted, Wade and Edgar simultaneously shouted, "What?"

Jack turned to Edgar. "I'm sorry, bud. I think what we're planning is way too dangerous, and you don't have the . . . you're not able to . . . well, shit, dude, you're a fucking dog now."

"So?"

"Well, what are you going to do if things get physical? Take a dump in their shoes?"

"It's a start."

"No. No way. You're staying with Wade."

"But," Wade said, his eyes wide and unflinching. "But . . . I'm not even supposed to—"

"Oh, come on, man," Jack said, "Stop being such a little bitch."

"Yeah," Edgar said as he scratched his ear with a hind leg, "there's no reason to be speciesist for fuck's sake."

"Hey . . . I don't think that's fair to—"

"Decision's final," Jack said. "Deal with it. Please. Both of you. We've got to have some semblance of teamwork here if we're going to make shit happen."

Wade sighed. Jack knew his friend was horrible at arguing his points. Any point at all. He had no chance of winning this battle. The coke only made it worse. It made Wade paranoid. Jack could see it in his eyes.

"Fine," Wade said. "Fucking fine. Just keep me in the loop. Let me know where you're going and when. You'll need me eventually." Wade took a sip of scotch, then another, then laid out another rail. Jack glanced at the once half-full bottle, noticed there was barely a drip left now. Before Wade went in for a second snort, he added, "Just please help me find Carey after you take care of this."

"Of course. Or he'll turn up here eventually. He knows you love him. He's just in shock. He'll come back. I promise, man. We'll get this all sorted out and have him back to you good as new. Or . . . as old. Shit, you know what I mean."

Wade sniffled, perhaps from the coke, perhaps because he was crying, and touched his fingers to the top of Jack's hand. "Thanks. I appreciate the comfort, even if I don't believe it."

Edgar chuckled. "You guys are fucking sickening. Get a room."

Jack kicked Edgar. Just a light pop. Not hard enough to be cruel, but enough to make him a little grumpier.

"Have you heard from Lucas?" Jack asked. "Maybe Carey's with him."

Kat shuffled back into the room. She did not sit down again. She stood with her arms crossed.

"No," Wade said. "I tried to call him, but he didn't pick up."

"Keep trying."

"Can we go back to Hannah's now?" Kat asked, her voice mousy and maudlin. "Please. I'm really worried."

"Yeah," Jack said. "Of course. We'll go right now. We're done here." A beam of sunlight seeped through the blinds, briefly highlighting Kat's left eye. It was covered in a milky white haze. She saw him staring and looked away.

"Call me soon," Wade said. Jack gave him a thumbs up.

As they left, Jack noticed Edgar had hopped up onto Wade's velvet barrel chair. He shut the door softly, and the cursing on the other side soon ensued.

CHAPTER SEVENTEEN

GRADY STROLLED INTO The Crawling Pub at an hour far too early for anyone to be drinking for any other reason than utter despair. It was a cave inside, dark and damp. From the jukebox spewed an old hair metal power ballad he couldn't quite put his finger on. He spotted a hot piece of ass sitting alone in the corner booth. He knew immediately it was Carey.

Emphasis on *was*.

Before, when he was still Lucas, he had gone to the costume shop with his brother. They purchased their costumes together. He was certain Carey would no longer be the same, and his instincts did not fail him.

Anyone else in The Crawling Pub wasn't going to notice Carey for being anything other than a trim little twat now, but Grady knew better. He also decided the male pronoun was still appropriate to use in this case, at least in his thoughts. Carey was still technically his brother—Lucas's brother, even if he had a pair of grade A melons now. Some people would do serious jail time just to get a peek at them. Terrible, unspeakable deeds had been performed for far less. Clearly Carey hadn't asked to be blessed with breasts, but it could have been worse. It was a far cry from the putrid mess Kat Dyer was turning into. No matter how much of a dump life became, there was always someone who had some extra garbage piled upon them.

Carey's mascara was slightly smeared, as if he had been crying but had taken the time to try and fix it. It made him look as if he'd been out partying the night before and things had gone horribly wrong. Which, technically, was what had happened.

Grady guessed Wade had given Carey the boot. And he was probably right. Lucas's mind had given him access to everything he needed to now. Wade would have been completely disgusted to be in a relationship with a woman, however unreal that woman was. But their relationship had been strong before this morning. It was why he had come looking for his brother here. Where Wade had asked Carey to marry him a few months before. It looked like the wedding was probably off. Now Carey was dodging male bullets left and right, sending them and their complimentary drinks packing.

It was time for a fun little experiment.

Grady approached the booth, and Carey stole a few subtle glances at him, but Grady knew he would not be recognized. Not this time. He had no idea why this problem occurred with Hannah Harper. He saw it in her eyes, sensed it at the tip of her tongue, and then she confirmed his suspicions. She had known it was Lucas somehow, as if the transformation had not been 100% complete. But he had it under control now.

Not that he was even Lucas anymore. Not really. He was Grady fucking Sullivan. Or some tweaked combo of the two. Lucas's mind was still there, his memories and emotions mixing with Grady's like they were being pureed in a psycho smoothie. His new body was lankier, his face unnaturally chiseled so it was almost impossible to tell what race he was, and he had an irresistible mustache and perfect teeth now. He didn't miss his slight overbite one bit. In fact, he still felt bitterness toward his father for never getting it fixed even though they clearly had the money. A trip to the dentist had been on Lucas's tentative calendar for sometime in the coming months, but now it looked like it wasn't going to be necessary.

Before coming to The Crawling Pub, Grady had followed a young man who looked about the right size. Dressed in his Sunday best, most likely just coming from church. The man was smiling, confident. He seemed to feel safe and secure in his skin. He had no idea he was being followed. No idea he should have been afraid. No idea there was horrible danger lurking in broad daylight in Los Angeles. The man obviously hadn't lived here long.

Grady waited until the man headed down an unpopulated side street, then made his move. He choked the man until he passed out, then stabbed him in the side for good measure. He dragged the limp body down an alley and quickly removed the man's clothes, leaving him only in his boxers, socks, and undershirt. He'd likely live, assuming no major organs were punctured, but Grady wasn't hanging around to find out. It wasn't his problem anymore.

He got in his car, drove a few blocks over to the Astro Burger on Melrose, somehow managed to slither into the restroom without anyone noticing, then changed and washed Beth's dry blood from his face and hands. Slicked his hair back. It might not have been an authentic look the fans were used to, but Mr. Sullivan was a man of many looks, and he wanted to look presentable so he could blend into the real world, do some real damage. Plus, he sure as hell didn't need to get accosted by any delusional fan boys on the street. He made a mental note to steer clear of Grauman's Chinese Theatre, leave the cosplay and the photo ops to the Spidermen, Shreks, and Captain Jack Sparrows.

After making himself decent in the restroom, he went through the drive-thru and ordered a chili dog, no onions. He stashed his jumpsuit and work boots in his trunk, realizing he'd left his bowler's cap somewhere. At Hannah's house, most likely. He wouldn't be seeing that again.

Grady wondered if the world he now walked through was even the real world anymore, or had there been just enough of a tear in the fabric of reality to consider it a fantastical creation? Did it matter one way or the other as long as he was enjoying it? Fiction and fantasy were just alternate angles of reality. He'd swallow the pill and take the fantasy any day, Alice, if it meant he got to participate in a bit of the old ultra-violence. Burgess, Carroll, what was the difference? They were both limey literary wimps.

Now—in The Crawling Pub—Grady leered as he passed by Carey, then strolled over to the bar and ordered a Rum & Coke. It arrived quickly, and it was a horrible, watered-down mess.

He made googly eyes at Carey from across the pub, just to see what he would do. Grady almost laughed out loud when he thought he saw his brother blush. Sure looked like it. Probably didn't even realize it. Grady already had him eating out of the palm of his hand.

If he wanted to, he could play hard-to-get for just a bit while he finished his awful drink. He wished he had the other kind of coke right now. He could have really used a rail.

No more waiting. It was time for him to go hit on a young lady who was also his brother who was also gay. Was that the first time such a sentence had ever been pondered in the English language? It depended on what part of the country one lived in. Lucas didn't know, and neither did Grady. He didn't fraternize with hillbillies.

He swaggered over to Carey's booth and slid his way in with no regard for manners. He was of the belief that most women wanted a man who took charge. The type of man who made things happen when he wanted them to happen. Plenty wouldn't admit it, but it was just nature taking its course, and who was he to dispute Darwin? He saw no worth in being a wuss and begging *oh pretty please can I please have the privilege of sitting here and listening to you talk about babies and fashion and reality television about vapid housewives while I absently nod for an hour, please?*

Nope. If he was going to have to suffer through any of that business, it was going to be on his terms. Plus, he knew Carey wasn't going to want to talk about that crap anyway. He hadn't had enough time to truly acclimate himself to proper womanly ways. Grady was still curious to see where the conversation went, though. See if Carey could pull off his character as well as Lucas was channeling Grady. He doubted it. Wade was the theater guy. Carey was a track and field star. No one would have ever caught him at a fucking musical.

He decided to give a fake name, searching Lucas's brain and combining the first and last names of two of his other favorite famous cinematic serial killers.

"Hello," Grady said, "I'm Jason Bateman."

He realized too late someone just as famous, but decidedly less dangerous, already had a stronger claim to that name. Carey's eye twitched, maybe because he noticed, but also maybe because a bug flew in it. It didn't matter either way.

He offered his hand to Carey, then Carey extended his, and it was as soft as vanilla pudding. He was wearing silver sparkly polish on his nails. The devil was in the details.

"Hi . . . I'm . . . my name is Caroline. You can call me . . . uh . . . Carrie, though. I guess."

It was interesting how that worked out. There were more than a few gender-neutral names in the world. Tracey, Jamie, Ashley, Dana, Pat. Just a quick spelling switch could do the same for other names. *Carey, Carey, bo-berry, banana-fana fo-fairy.*

Grady turned on his seductive smile. As Lucas Lane, he definitely had his fair share of game, though he'd be the first to admit most ladies probably spread their legs for him solely because of the size of his bank account. However, being Grady Sullivan just gave him straight up panty-droppin' charm. He made a regular ladies' man like Ted Bundy look more like Marty Feldman.

"You have a boyfriend?" Carey flinched when Grady asked this. It must have been torturing him to stir up thoughts of Wade. It was even better than when they were kids and Lucas used to tell Carey the Boogeyman would get him.

Apparently Lucas hadn't been lying after all.

"No . . . not anymore. Um . . . we broke up recently." His voice was a husky whisper, just on the verge of quivering. His new feminine tone seemed to be achieved by affecting his natural voice, which had always been somewhat effeminate. Grady almost felt sorry for him. *Almost* because he had to play some tricks with his voice as well. It wasn't like Lucas had ever been a Barry White or anything like that, but his voice was at least slightly smooth before. Now it had an itty-bitty squeak to it, like he was chewing on a dog toy when speaking. A small price to pay to transform into an American icon.

He wasn't sure if the people who considered Grady Sullivan an American icon were exactly trustworthy or even mentally stable, but Lucas was one of those miscreants, too, so he figured they couldn't all be bad.

"Well, his loss is my gain, then." Not an ounce of bashfulness or modesty in his mind and body. No way, no how.

In less than ten minutes they were off to Carey's apartment. It was almost too easy. On Friday afternoon, Lucas had dropped his car off for deluxe detailing, and it wasn't scheduled for pickup until Monday. He was using a rental for now. Carey wouldn't have a clue. However, Grady had to lie and say his place (he called it his "pad") was being fumigated and that he was crashing at a friend's. Carey obviously knew where Lucas lived, and things would have gotten a bit too complicated. He didn't need that, no siree, Bob.

Most people would likely wonder what sort of sick bastard took home a woman who was also his brother who was also gay (Grady decided he needed to copyright that phrase, make some t-shirts and bumper stickers). Grady briefly pondered if incest had been a secret desire hiding in the blackest caverns of Lucas's mind. Once he dug deep into his psyche, he realized Lucas had clear misgivings about the situation, which Grady allayed. He claimed his new body no longer shared blood with Carey. Whether or not this was true, he could not prove, but it eased his brain brother's fears, so he stood behind the claim.

However, whether they would admit to it or not, most people were lookie-loos, a quality that was considerably amplified if it involved senseless violence. Anyone who had ever willingly gone to see *Emancipation Day Part III* or any of its sequels more than likely wanted something bad to happen. Something very awful, something that would make their sphincters shrink and their stomachs churn. They probably got their jollies from it just as much as Grady did, if not more. Then they went back to their regularly scheduled program of kiddie soccer games, sautéed green beans, pop-country tunes, watered-down wine coolers, and Feng Shui. Shame on the sickos. Their mothers would disown them.

Grady would deliver the goods. It'd be just like in the movies, only his eyes would be the camera. He only wished he could share it with his loyal fans.

———— ◆ ————

Carey's apartment was more or less Wade-free, though Grady caught Carey grabbing a framed photo of the formerly happy couple and tossing it in a drawer. While Carey was doing this, Grady checked out the closet. Only a couple of dresses and a long line of arguably manly pants and shirts. Out with the old and in with the new. He'd somehow found the time to get a little shopping in. Carey always was a shopper. Or it's possible the dresses were older. Last night wasn't the first time Carey had done drag.

Carey hustled over and slid the closet door shut, shooting Grady a half-worried glance. Grady got the message. A girl needed her privacy.

"Sorry . . . uh, my ex hasn't come back to pick up the rest of his clothes and most of my stuff is at the cleaner's right now. We were about to move in together before we broke up. That's why I have all these boxes." His brother was a lot sharper than he'd ever given him credit for. Thinking on his itty-bitty tippy toes. A lie that relied on pieces of truth.

Grady approached Carey, took a hunk of his silky hair, and twirled it into a ringlet around his finger. No one ever accused him of not being flirty. He was close enough to Carey now that he could smell something like coconut. Carey looked like he was about to say something, but Grady placed a finger across his lips. *Hush, little baby, don't say a word.* He didn't need to say anything, though. Grady could see the lust in his eyes, the yearning for a meaningless fuck with some random joker he met in a pub. The perfect rebound. Someone with whom to temporarily forget the horrors of today, even though there were far greater horrors to come. Grady thought he had heard somewhere that it was the Gay Holy Grail to bag a straight guy. Seemed like Carey had the perfect set-up for that now.

Carey stroked Grady's thigh, and the friction between slacks and skin was marvelous. His hand moved closer to Grady's already-erect prick. Carey applied more pressure, a squeeze, a tug, a light scratch across the length of the shaft, and Grady moaned. Carey leaned for a kiss, but Grady pulled back.

"I don't do kisses," Grady said. Seemed like a really unromantic thing to mention in the heat of the moment, but this moment was not meant to make anyone feel all fuzzy inside. Lucas had never been able to hang with saliva, a trait that Grady now inherited. Saliva was too intimate. He did not wish to share anyone's leftover food particles.

Carey paused, then slid the straps of his dress down his shoulders and tugged it at the waist. The fabric was loose enough that it glided down his body and left him only in his unmentionables. Grady was impressed. Considering Carey had no choice when he shifted sexes, he should have felt fortunate that he at least got to become a full-blown fox. After all, he could have gone as Tipper Gore for Halloween. And Grady would have been at the other side of town while Carey was suffering through that misfortune alone.

Grady's clothes were off now as well, and he wasn't sure how or when that happened. He felt a breeze coming in from the window. It tickled his scrotum. After a blazing October they were finally getting a slight chill in Los Angeles. Of course, southern California's version of cold was like summer taking a power nap.

In the mirror he noticed a detail he hadn't seen before. A tattoo on his left shoulder blade, just like Grady in the movies. Porky from the Looney Tunes cartoons, a caption below it that said SQUEAL LIKE A PIG '72. Classy.

Grady and Carey got down to business. They played Hide the Salami. The cucumber fit in the oyster and went Boom, Boom, Boom. To be honest it wasn't one of his top twenty greatest lays. Not as Lucas, nor as Grady. Not even close. But it helped clear his mind.

They lay together on the bed, after the deed was done. Grady's flaccid wang hung to one side like a deflated balloon. Carey smoked a slim, the covers pulled up above his chest.

The real fun was about to begin.

"So Carey," Grady said, trying to hold back his goblin glee, "remember that time you lit a match and threw it at a tree and it caught on fire?" Carey's arm was pressed against his, and Grady felt it lock up. He swore he felt it go cold. Grady grinned so wide that his jaw throbbed.

"What are you—"

"And I never told Mom, either. You made me promise and I stuck to it. Scout's honor. All that shit. It wasn't any worse than— remember the time you brought home that frog in the jar? You left it out on the side of the garage in the middle of August and forgot about it. It took us a while to figure out what the hell the smell was, but—"

Carey dropped the lit cigarette on the bed. "What the fuck? How would you know about that? Who have you been talking to? Who put you up to this?" He grabbed the cigarette back up before it had the chance to cause any major damage, then smooshed it into an ashtray on the nightstand and beat at the sheets for good measure. "How do you know I'm . . ."

"It's me, Carey. Lucas. Sort of."

Carey looked right at him with those beautiful baby eyes. He was in denial, and he was not hiding it well. He slid off the bed, inched toward the door. But Grady knew he had him cornered. Carey wasn't going to just dash out into the street in his brand new birthday suit.

Grady had to make sure Carey knew exactly what was going on before he killed him. It wouldn't have been half as fun without this step. It was just fucking poetic. He felt like the Grindhouse Shakespeare.

He lunged, and Carey sprinted into the hallway before he could grab him. Grady grabbed a lamp as he ran out of the room, ripping the plug from its socket. Carey was in the kitchen now. His brother-turned-sister was fast, but Grady was faster. Just as Carey reached for a cast-iron pan hanging from the pot rack, Grady swung the lamp with monstrous force. It connected with Carey's head with a loud crack and knocked him to the floor.

Carey stumbled, tried to get up, but Grady went straight for the throat. Carey might have had a slight chance if he was still in his male body, but his muscles were basically nonexistent now. A fit bird, for certain, but far from a formidable athlete. Grady squeezed so tight that Carey couldn't even eke out a squeal, much less a scream. That was fine. Grady preferred a silent kill. It gave him time to gather his thoughts, figure out what his next move was.

He tightened his grip even more, then something cracked. Carey's body stopped struggling, shifted to a slight twitch. Done and done. It was over much faster than Grady would have liked. It was never a good idea to blow your wad too early. Nobody liked a minute man.

Grady let Carey's body drop, then he kneeled down and played with his brother's nipples a little bit. Tune in Tokyo. Carey sure as hell wasn't going to care anymore. And they were such nice nipples. Grady felt it a shame to let them go to waste.

So he removed them. Sliced them off cleanly. Put them in his pocket. He'd find a use for them later.

Grady's next stop was an important one. He was looking forward to it.

He couldn't wait to show them the monster they created.

CHAPTER EIGHTEEN

KAT HADN'T FELT well since she'd started rotting, but that was to be expected. Transforming into the equivalent of a soggy corpse didn't feel the same as receiving a foot massage with soothing minty oils. She wondered how much time she had before she was reduced to nothing more than a blob, worrying her brain would still be operating as normal after the fact. She would be unable to move, to breathe, to be, yet she would still be able to think. She felt like she'd been slowly withering away for weeks, but Hannah's Halloween party was just last night. Perception of time changed drastically when life hung in the balance.

Hannah. Poor Hannah. By Kat's side like a Siamese twin for so many years and now . . . .just gone. Sliced and diced by the hands of an unknown maniac. Kat couldn't stop thinking about her butchered best friend. Jack had done his best to comfort her, but Kat was inconsolable. She couldn't get the image out of her head, and she didn't think she ever would. Seeing Jonah cradling Hannah's limp, butchered body as if he could somehow revive her with a warm embrace.

The blood . . . oh God, the blood. Jack and Jonah had cleaned it as best they could, scrubbing it and soaping it to the point that it looked like a few bottles of wine might have crashed to the concrete. Jack and Jonah wrapped Hannah's body in ghost-white towels that were probably worth more than Kat's monthly rent and took her to

the cabana, out of the sun. Kat had curled herself into a ball while
the boys worked. She couldn't deal. She closed her eyes and
pretended for just a moment that life was not the brutal hell it had
become. In her mind, she was a child again. Before she ever knew
Hannah existed. Before Jack. Before any of them even mattered. No
responsibilities, no repercussions. It was a nice lie while it lasted.

Kat wanted to scream at Jack and Jonah, tell them they had to
do something, they had to call the cops. But that would just make
her a hypocrite. And the cops couldn't bring Hannah back.

Nothing could.

Except.

Maybe.

If they were right about Cosmo's and the people there were
willing and able to change her, Edgar, and everyone else back to
normal, it wasn't too much of a stretch to think they dabbled in
bringing people back from the dead. She had to hold on to some
thread of hope, even if that thread was thin and made of old
pantyhose.

She hoped Hannah's parents would not find their daughter like
this, that they would not return home and notice the stains and the
growing smell in the cabana. But it was unlikely. Her father was in
Spain overseeing preliminary shoots on a new Kirk Dietrich film. He
was unreachable. And Mrs. Harper likely wouldn't be home for some
time. "Late brunch and shopping trip" was common code for a
weeklong tryst with one of her many lovers.

Once, when she and Hannah had barely turned eighteen, they
had taken a trip down to Rosarito and drank themselves into
oblivion over a three-day weekend. Kat had lied to her parents,
claiming they were camping at Big Bear Lake, but Hannah hadn't
even told her parents she was leaving for lunch.

She knew deep down that Mr. and Mrs. Harper wouldn't even
notice Hannah was gone. Not anytime soon, if ever.

When the boys were done with their dark duty, Jonah was given
the task of making the phone calls Hannah was unable to complete.
Jack gave him a list, a time, a place. The plans were in motion.

Kat had to try to stop thinking about Hannah, if only for the fact
that her salty tears were burning the left side of her face.

She wiped the wetness with the back of her arm. A scabby flap of skin the size of a small sticky note tore away. She felt a pinch and squealed, then winced when she saw a thick, pasty puddle of grey pus oozing from the fresh wound. She heaved for a moment, then gathered her composure and scrambled for something to stop the seepage. She found a dirty T-shirt on the floor and wrapped it around her arm, tight like a tourniquet.

She grabbed a bottle from her nightstand, took a sip of lukewarm beer, then lit a stick of Nag Champa to mask the wretched scents surrounding her. Her bedroom smelled faintly like a family of rats died in the walls, and she wondered how much of the aroma might be coming from her own body. She decided to let the incense do its job as best it could, and she left the bedroom.

In her tiny living room, barely the size of most normal people's closets, Jack slept and snored on her couch. He was exhausted, and he had told her to give him no more than an hour for a quick nap, then they needed to get ahold of everyone and set a time to meet at Cosmo's. She had let him sleep longer. It was almost dark now.

The light of the television flashed manically throughout the room, though the volume was muted. For a moment she thought she was watching an episode of *Friends*, but then she wondered why Joey was hanging out with a chimp in a baseball uniform. She shrugged and shut the television off. It made a loud pop. Kat cringed, but Jack did not stir.

Jack's bare, shockingly white long legs dangled over the arm of the couch with dead weight. He wore a tank top, boxers, and nothing else. She had left him a ratty blanket, but it remained folded next to the couch. The strange autumn heat had made blankets only necessary for true masochists. Kat couldn't help but notice Jack was impressively erect beneath his underwear. The fabric barely contained the stiff meat within.

She looked away but didn't. She wondered if a tempting dream caused this unintended indiscretion, or if it was merely the result of uncontrollable young male hormones. Either way, she was intrigued by the display. And, really, as embarrassed as she was, there was no harm in looking. Admiring the spectacle from afar. It was something to focus on, to use as a distraction, to lust after in the face of despair.

It was in this moment, seeing her longtime friend so vulnerable and so pure in his unabashed masculinity, that Kat realized she was truly in love with him. She had known this to be true almost since the first moment they met, but always let the thought hide deep in the furthest corridors of her mind. Maybe it never mattered until now. Perhaps the urgency of their current situation forced the truth out, but she realized she might not have much time left to pursue her feelings. Just yesterday, she had planned on putting off saying anything until she was of ancient age and on life support, when she would finally profess her love in Morse code by blinking her elderly eyes.

And Jack hadn't treated her any differently in these past two days. Or, at least, he'd put on a performance worthy of Oscar consideration. Either way, he was what she needed. Before and after.

She couldn't resist anymore. Maybe it was the booze, but staring wasn't enough. She took the final swig from her bottle and set it on the TV stand. Using the fingers on her right hand—the ones that still looked and felt somewhat normal, she brushed against the tip of Jack's penis. He squeaked and moaned and Kat realized the absolute power she had over him, even when he was asleep, even in her current form. The pure power of sex. It was certainly not the only power women had over men, but it might be the most potent. Kat felt conflicted about this possibility, but figured she'd save the feminism for another day.

She shifted the fly of Jack's boxers and his flesh slipped out. Jack's penis was far from the first she had ever seen up close, but it was arguably one of the nicest, and certainly the first she ever wanted to tie a pretty bow around, just so she had an excuse to untie it again. She kneeled down to get a closer look. Smooth and curved like a banana, its head round like a *Stahlhelm*. She forgot all about her pain and her rot and let the deviant devil on her shoulder take over. She let herself become a slave to prurient desire.

"Kat?"

Her heart slid out her colon. She couldn't move, couldn't even breathe.

"Kat . . . what are you . . . what are you doing?"

A horn honked outside, as if the driver intended to mock her. Jack wouldn't be dreaming for long. She maybe had milliseconds to make the right choices about how the rest of the scene went down.

"Um . . . I'm . . . just . . . nothing?"

She found the bravery within her to face Jack head-on. She could still see fine out of her right eye. Her left eye was glazed, bulging, near useless. Jack was still waking up. Groggy, innocent eyes. She probably still had time to act as if she had dropped something and was just kneeling back to pick it up and maybe, just maybe he'd buy the story.

There was only one problem: she had nothing to drop. There would be nothing to pick up. If only there were a way to turn her pride into a tangible thing.

They stared at each other in silence. Kat's lips felt like sandpaper when pressed together. She did her best to moisten them with the tip of her tongue. The roughness on the left side stung her tongue, and she tasted something sour. Her eyes darted back and forth from Jack's face to his penis. She couldn't help it. Jack's eyes darted in the same general direction. They soon looked back in forth in unison, as if watching an intense Ping-Pong match. He smirked. Awkwardly, not with the cocky confidence some young men might.

"God, I want to kiss you," Kat said. She was not sure who was saying that. It sounded like her. But she would never say those words. Not in fifty lifetimes. Certainly not now. She wondered if there might be a rewind button somewhere that she could press. Of course not. That would be too convenient. "Would that . . . would that be okay?"

"You what?"

"You heard me."

"You want to—"

"Down there."

Jack eyes widened. He glanced back in the direction of his penis. Kat followed his gaze, for clarification. When he turned back to look at her again, Kat could see in his eyes that he was both conflicted and terrified, struggling to come up with something kind to say to the melting creature in front of him. He shifted his penis, still erect, back into his boxers. Kat looked away again, mortified. She wanted to make the situation less awkward, but realized too late she was probably doing just the opposite. There was no escape from awkward in this room, not in this moment. This could have been a perfect moment before today, something they could have laughed about years from now, but now it was a sickening farce.

"Kat, I don't think . . . we can't wait any longer. You need help. You need a doctor. You're not going to make it until the morning. I think . . . fuck. I think it's spreading."

"It's too late for me anyway. Wouldn't matter if we went to a doctor now even if I wanted to. Don't sugarcoat it."

Jack's eyes welled with tears. "Goddammit, Kat! Why won't you let me help you?" He hopped off the couch, paced wildly around the room. "Fuck, I need a cigarette."

Kat looked away. It was time to tell him the truth.

"Jack, there's something I need to talk to you about."

Jack stopped pacing, focused all of his attention on Kat. "What's wrong?"

"I haven't been to a doctor since I was little. Since I was twelve."

"What? Why? Your folks are insured, aren't they? Don't you have insurance through work?

"Yes they do, and no I don't. That's not the point."

"You could have come to me if you needed money. I would have at least paid for you to go for a checkup or whatever. Jesus. You know that, right?"

Kat nodded. "You're not getting it, though. That's not what I mean." She crouched, then sat, then cried. It was too late to turn back.

Jack sat next to her, lightly grabbing her good hand.

"Kat, what is it? You can tell me anything." In this moment, life was almost normal again. It was no longer man speaking to monster. It was one lost soul reaching out to another, willing to give her anything. No conditions.

She hesitated, gathered some of her composure. "I've never told anyone else this. Except . . . except Hannah." Speaking her friend's name sent her into minor hysterics again. She didn't think she could go through with this. She didn't want any of this. She didn't want to live anymore if it meant her body would have to be filled with so much crushing pain.

Jack squeezed her hand tighter. Not too tight. Just enough. "It's okay. I'm here, Kat. I love you. Nothing changes that." It was spoken so casually, perhaps in the heat of the moment, but Kat knew that was what made it honest.

"My doctor. He . . . "

"Take your time. It's just you and me here."

"When I was a kid . . . my doctor. Dr. Hamlin. He . . . he . . . oh, God. Fuckfuckfuck."

She couldn't say it.

She didn't have to.

Jack carefully placed a finger to the right side of her lips, where the flesh was still somewhat normal, then leaned in and kissed her gently with the same side of his lips. Corner to corner.

"Don't worry," he said. "I won't ever let anyone hurt you like that again. I can't change the past, but I'm here now. And I won't stop being here. I promise."

Kat smiled. It was sincere. Maybe it was the last smile she would experience in her short life, but it was the most genuine. She wished she still looked the way she looked before Halloween, when she might not have been perfect but was at least whole. Young and dumb, covered in soft, milky skin. She could have been his then and still could be now. As long as he kept his eyes closed, she could be an unforgettable dream rather than a persistent, haunting nightmare.

"You don't have to look at me," she said. "I know I'm fucking hideous."

"Maybe in Bizarro World, but here in Van Nuys it's a different story."

Kat let loose a tiny laugh that transformed into an equally tiny cry. It was a strangely sweet sentiment, even if it was an obvious lie. But it was why Kat loved Jack. He would do anything to make her feel needed. He had the innate ability to convince her to forget just how cruel the world could be. She stood up, deciding to be brave again. She never really cared for the trite acronym YOLO, but right now she understood its sentiments and appreciated what it stood for. It made more sense now that her life was truly on the line, when she could very well be in the grave soon, the bitter rain soaking into her nicest clothes, the soil pressing its weight upon her bones, the worms already burrowing through her skull and whispering sweet nothings into her ear.

"Turn away for a second."

Jack did.

She removed her hoodie and tossed it to the ground, then pulled down her jeans. She was worried she might not be able to remove her dress, which was now bunched up and wrinkled. She had yet to attempt it. Technically, it was part of the costume. But off it came, revealing a rough road map of leprous flesh. Her left breast was a flat, drooping pancake covered in inflamed sores. Her right was perky, near immaculate. She lay down on the couch, then grabbed the blanket from the floor and spread it over her left side, covering as much of the rot as she could. There was nothing that could be done about the patches that had started to spread to her right side. It would have to do.

"Okay."

Jack turned back around. She begged him to come closer. He did. This was likely their only chance to do what they were always meant to do together. Or as close as they'd ever be allowed to now.

He ran his fingers lightly over the sections of her skin that were still smooth, from ankle to ear, then returned to her chest. He looked at her, she nodded, and he leaned in, suckling at her raw exposed breast like a hungry newborn.

She felt chills down her right side and a mixture of sweat and possibly something disgustingly juicy exuding underneath the blanket on her left side. She reached down and caressed Jack's cock, at first without grace, but as the seconds passed her strokes became more confident. His moans of pleasure informed her movements. She tried not to think about the horrors she was subjecting him to. He looked a little uncomfortable, but sex was never like it was in the movies. The soundtrack was rarely appropriate, the passion was sometimes accompanied by garlic breath, flatulence, and dingle berries, and the end result was a sticky mess.

Kat was about to climax from Jack's ravenous attack on her breast. It was a sensation like none she had experienced before. Just a few seconds more and she would be in ecstasy. So close.

Suddenly she felt a tender, tearing pain. She released her grip on Jack.

Jack's body froze for a moment, then he pulled his face away from her breast. He coughed and gagged and spit something into his hand. It looked like a Jujube.

They both breathed heavily. Kat felt a tingling in the nerves at the tips of her breast. The room was otherwise so quiet that their breaths might have been breaking some sort of noise ordinance. They both stared with empty expressions at the little nub sitting in the middle of Jack's palm.

"Holy shit," Jack said. "Holy mother of fuck."

Kat's nipple.

From her good side.

Kat now understood all too well why Hannah used to always tell her romance was overrated.

CHAPTER NINETEEN

GRADY SNIFFED THROUGH the barely open crack of the window. He crouched atop a dull green transformer box, just enough to stay out of sight, hidden from the street behind a mass of foliage. The outside of the window was caked in bug guts and dirt spread thin by long forgotten rains. Through the crack he could smell the mix of incense and piña colada spray Kat Dyer was using to mask the scent of her rot. Her bedroom was like the Tiki Room of Death.

Jack Lantin mumbled to Kat, and Grady couldn't understand his words because they were crushed by music with loud guitars, but not the kind of loud guitars he (or Lucas for that matter) liked. In Grady's mind, guitars were the truest extension of the mighty cock, axes that should only be wielded by emaciated men squeezed into spandex and leather, painted with womanly war paint. Songs about drinking and fucking and getting away with petty crimes, not nonsensical, badly written poetry that, in many cases, was actually covering the same essential subject matter.

Kat sobbed, or at least it appeared that way, and the sound was like a sweet lullaby to Grady. He thought of the arias he could compose were he to record her cries. Mix it down, put it in a loop, add an obnoxiously infectious beat to her endless, anguished tears.

He also realized how tired he was. It had been a long, busy day since being reborn. He had been subsisting solely on his will to kill, but even that was not enough. He was, after all, still human. Even if the human he had become was a fictional character capable of committing multiple atrocities, he still craved his Ralph Lauren pillow, his Euro Top mattress. Sleep was still his master, he its submissive dog. But first he had to complete his duties for the night. He needed to draw blood, and plenty of it. Then, and only then, would he allow himself a few moments of rest.

Something rustled in the bushes behind him.

"Hey assmuncher . . . whatcha doin'?" Grady's heart leaped, and it was the first time since his metamorphosis that he realized he could still experience fear. He almost fell off the transformer, and his body made a deafening BANG as it slammed against the cold steel. He winced at the noise and spun around to see a small boy squinting at him. Grady moved to a sitting position. He was back in his filthy jumpsuit now, and it felt much more comfortable than the suit he was wearing when he seduced Carey. He kept his hands folded atop his lap to appear less threatening, less predatory. There wasn't much he could do to steer the child's attention from the bloodstains.

The boy stood bowlegged, as if he were attempting to find relief from an especially pesky hemorrhoid.

"None of your business, twerp. Get lost." Grady nodded his head in the direction he guessed the boy had come from. He didn't give two squirts which direction the brat went so long as he started putting one foot in front of the other.

"What the fuck is a twerp, loser? Better cut the shit 'fore I call up the po-po."

Grady was impressed with the kid's potty mouth and his apparent nuts of iron. Reminded him of a boy he once knew. A boy he once was. A decade and some change had really done some damage to his soul.

"Well, if you really need to know what the hell I'm doing . . . I'm, uh . . . well, I locked myself out of my apartment and I'm trying to get back in. Can't you see? So scram, why don'tcha?"

"Nu-uh. You don't live there. That little blondie *chica* with the sweet chi-chis, that's her place. I seen her on Halloween."

Grady grinned. A little too wide. He was really starting to like this kid. Maybe his choice of women was a bit suspect considering Kat's current condition, but still . . . he had plenty of time to develop a more refined taste. Well, he would have had plenty of time under different circumstances. It was too bad Grady was going to have to kill him.

Grady kept smiling, so sweetly his teeth could have been made of hard candy.

He reached into his pocket, felt the stiff steel of his knife.

He stood up from the transformer, took one step forward.

"Danny!" A motherly voice echoed from two buildings down. Grady had been correct about the direction the boy had come from. "*Ándale, mijo!*"

"*Hijo de puta,*" little Danny said. He spit off to the side, then pointed at Grady as if to imply "next time" and skittered off in zigzag motion. Grady assumed the boy would soon be brushing his teeth for 30 seconds less than he should, heading to bed, and dreaming of a naked woman he once saw through the static of the cable programming his family couldn't afford.

Grady leaned back against the transformer, then adjusted back into his previous crouching position and peeked through the window again. Jack and Kat were still talking, none the wiser. He was relieved the ruckus had not blown his cover.

He could see traces of Kat's scabby skin. He wished he could just reach in and peel a small section off. It would have almost been worth being exposed to hear her squeal, to rip the chunk free like a crusty Band-Aid, to see the once-trapped blood seep through mere seconds later, the platelets and white blood cells already working toward coagulation. He'd even consider taking a nibble of the scab, even though it would probably taste like a stale piece of artisan jerky with too much iron. Again, probably worth it. He was willing to try just about anything once.

Through the crack, it looked like Jack was holding Kat close to him now. Not like a lover, not like a friend. Somewhere in the unclassifiable void between. Kat was still sobbing, but the sounds were softer now. Whatever pain had taken hold of her was subsiding.

But not for long.

Grady slid a shiny hunter's knife out from his front pocket. It was brand new. He preferred not to use the same weapon twice if he could help it. He also preferred to be more creative when he had more time and resources at his disposal, but the hunter's knife would have to do this time. And he would have to head for Jack first because he would be the more formidable foe of the two. Only because he was not falling apart at the seams like poor ole Kat.

He placed the knife between his teeth, resembling an Argentinian tango dancer clutching a rose's stem, then set his fingers under the edge of the window and lifted. Tried to. Failed. It would not budge. He needed to put his back into it. His fingers were only so strong. He had no choice. He had to go into beast mode to get the window to budge.

And budge it did, without so much as a warning. The lower sash smashed into the head of the frame with a giant THUNK. Glass shards of varying sizes rained down on Grady's head.

Things were not going as planned.

———— ◆ ————

The music was playing just a wee bit too loud in Kat's bedroom, so much so that her crappy speakers were vibrating like a wet fart. But Kat didn't mind. She wanted there to be noise in the room, as thick as three layers of steel, because silence would only draw attention to the horrific event that transpired less than thirty minutes ago.

Until today, Kat had not been aware a person could fall apart both emotionally *and* physically. Until this evening, she had not been privy to the intimate relationship between copulation and obliteration.

"I don't even know what to do," Jack said, shrugging as if he needed to emphasize the obvious. "We've got to figure out a way to fix you. I mean . . . fix everybody, yeah, but . . . but mostly fix you. Christ, I need a smoke. I haven't had a fucking cigarette all day. You don't happen to have one, do you? Did I ask you that already?"

Kat shook her head side-to-side in answer to the first question, then nodded to the second. She wondered if there were even tools on this earth capable of fixing her. Jack had thought on his toes, quickly rushing to the kitchen to seal her nipple up in a Ziploc baggie and toss it in the freezer. But it was probably a useless gesture. Eventually she would lose more parts, far too many to keep on ice in such a small space. All the king's horses and all the king's men would rather shit on a public toilet without the protection of a seat cover than risk touching her to put her back together again.

It felt like her bedroom was swallowing her whole. She wished that were the reality. A simple solution to a complex problem. She lit a vanilla candle, partially to further mask what she feared was her own progressively rotting scent, partially just to give her hands something to do. She didn't care that it would cause yummy aroma overload in the room. It was better than the alternative.

"There's nothing that can be done, Jack. I'm lost. I'm dyi—"

"No. No way. Don't say that. I just talked to Jonah. Once I get back in touch with Wade we're going to get everyone together, and . . . and we'll go to that fucking Cosmo's place and sort this shit out. I promise you. We'll fix this. I'll fix it on my own if I have to."

Fix fix fix. It's all Jack could say anymore. Kat continued to repeat the word in her mind like a mantra for the mentally deranged. The word lost all definition. It became instinct. Phonetic nonsense. Fix ficks ficts.

Kat thought she heard a crash or a bump or a rustle outside her window, but realized it was probably just the cacophony of the music, or a homeless guy trying to find a spot to crash for the night. She couldn't think straight, couldn't discern between what was real and what was fake and if it mattered either way at this point. Sounds were just auditory illusions, reality was just a fable concocted by a sadist, and love was just a lie perpetuated in hopes the human race would continue to mindlessly procreate.

It was at this moment that Jack pulled Kat close to him. And, despite her normally impeccable judgment, she let him. He did not speak. His warm body soothed her, but only because she allowed it to. And only because they were both fully clothed. Kat never wanted to be naked again. Any further instances of flesh against flesh were not an option in the foreseeable future. If it meant never showering for the rest of her life, just caking herself with the daily buildup of sweat and filth . . . well, she was ready to face that future. She figured it'd be a short-lived future anyway. She wasn't risking much.

But now she was certain she heard something outside the window. At the window. Tapping, scratching, perhaps even some cursing. She subtly curved her head around Jack's shoulder to take a peek.

"Jack, do you hear someth—"

The window flew open and the glass broke in one swift motion. Kat yelped.

Jack let go of her and pivoted around to face the window. He yelled "What the fuck?" Nothing else would have been more appropriate in this situation.

A body hung forward over the window. But it was not a dead body. Just a temporarily stunned one.

"Well, screw me sideways with a cheese grater," the body in the window said. He lifted his head slowly. Small shards of glass were almost strategically wedged into different sections of his face. One shard dangled mere millimeters from his left eye. Thin rivers of blood trickled like wayward tears. Kat had to squint before she realized she recognized the bloody face. Or recognized the face that used to be attached to what this body used to be. The man behind the costume.

"L-Lucas? Is that you?"

The Guy She Thought Was Lucas spit a dark globule of phlegm and blood and looked Kat deep in the eye. He frowned when he heard the name. "How did you . . . you . . . Goddammit!" He turned his frown upside down. He looked like he wanted to laugh but was showing restraint. And she knew without a doubt in her soul, despite the fact that this man looked basically nothing like Lucas, that it was definitely him. It made zero sense that she knew this, but she knew nevertheless. His reaction made it indisputable fact.

"Almost only counts in horseshoes and hand grenades," he continued, "but I'll let you slide this time. Lucas left town. Say hello to Grady Sullivan, you disgusting little bitch." He attempted to lift himself from the sill, but he didn't have a chance in hell because Jack rushed to the window and pulled him through the window like a sack of potatoes. Grady howled, likely due to being dragged across broken glass, but his painful wail ended in hiccupping giggles.

Jack threw himself between Kat and Grady, steadied himself for what was certain to be a dangerous encounter. "It is Lucas, Kat. Was Lucas. This was the costume he was wearing last night."

Grady was on all fours now. "Which one of you jokers wants to die first?" he asked. "I need a challenge. Baby Beth was too simple."

Kat gasped.

"And poor sister—I mean brother—Carey was a dead fuck." Grady was kneeling now. He moved his hips in a pumping motion.

"Jesus fucking Christ," Jack said. "No. No, man. You killed Carey? What the hell is wrong with you?"

Grady's voice turned squeakier. "Nothing's wrong, shithead. I've just turned over a new leaf. Everything's hunky dory. Tee-hee! Ho-ha!"

"Oh my God," Kat said. "It was you. Hannah. You sick motherfucking bastard! You killed Hannah, too, didn't you?"

Grady lit up at the mention of Hannah's name. "Mmm, mmm, mmm, sweet slutty little tuna meat. Best fish I ever tasted." Kat summoned all the strength she had, then lunged at Grady, but Jack turned and stopped her. He grabbed her arm, and she felt a piece of skin tear away, slightly dulled by the soft cotton of her sweatshirt. She was on the verge of hyperventilating.

Kat squinted over Jack's shoulder. There was something on the floor in front of Grady. Something shiny and silvery. She opened her mouth to scream to Jack, but the sound took too long to travel. It was in Grady's hand now. Grady pushed himself up with his free hand and swiped a hunting knife at Jack with bestial rage. Jack's good reflexes allowed him to move just in time to miss the brunt of the slash. The slice on his arm was not deep, but it still bled. A spray of red patterned across the light grey carpet. Kat absently thought that between this and however many pints were pouring out of Grady, she definitely wasn't getting her deposit back when she moved.

If she lived long enough to move.

"Kat!" Jack yelled, putting pressure on his arm, but ready to remove his hand to use his good arm if and when he needed it. "Run! Get out of here! I've got this!"

And run she did. But not to leave. She ran to her kitchen, as quickly as her weak, sloppy body would let her, and for the first time in her life she was thankful she could only afford a tiny apartment. It took a quick five steps for her to get from point A to point B.

She hunted through yellowed menus and expired coupons and frayed rubber bands for a few seconds before she realized she was digging through her junk drawer. Jack and Grady grunted and hollered in the next room, and she thought she heard a lamp break. She slid open the drawer next to the junk drawer and saw the stinging gleam of sharp, never-used gourmet knives, a gift from her parents when she first left home.

She was no idiot, at least not tonight.

She grabbed two knives. The biggest two.

When she returned to her room, Grady was straddling Jack, using all of his strength to drive his hunting knife toward Jack's face. The veins in Jack's arms were like little blue speed bumps. His glasses were cracked. His fingers were bleeding.

She also saw it was not a lamp that had broken. It was the glass that surrounded her vanilla candle. In the midst of their struggle they had knocked the candle off her vanity, and it somehow managed to land on the only portion of her bedroom floor that hadn't made the cut for wall-to-wall carpeting. Even less fortunately, the still-lit wick was pointed at a small pile of dirty laundry in the corner. One of her faded pink ankle socks caught the tip of the flame and lit. The rest of the laundry soon followed suit.

Kat screamed in frustration. She had no time to hesitate, but she also had so little strength. She had one move in her, and it had to count. She charged at the two young men and thrust the larger of the two knives into Grady's left buttock. It went a couple of inches deep, and she removed it quickly. Grady made a gurgling noise and released his grip on Jack, but not on his own knife. Jack took advantage of this momentary distraction and tackled Grady. His glasses went flying, and he shoved Grady's head into the dirty laundry flames. Whether accidentally or intentionally, Kat couldn't tell. But it was a blessing either way, one that Jack seemed to realize. He pressed Grady's head down and held it in the flame as long as he could. Grady shrieked like an otherworldly creature as his hair caught the flame. Jack's fingers touched the fire, and he threw his hands back and yelped. Grady patted wildly at his head, finally dropping the knife. One of his flailing legs connected directly with Jack's crotch and Jack relinquished control.

"Sunuvabitchfuckcuntlickadick," Grady yelled as he shoved Jack away. "What the fuck did you do to me?" He seemed to realize he had lost this battle. He was in retreat mode. He continued batting at what was left of his hair, putting out the remaining flames. His eyebrows were mostly singed away. The skin on his face was pink. He looked toward the doorway that could lead him in the direction of freedom, but Kat stood hard, clutching her two knives—one bloody, one clean. She wouldn't be able to stop him if he decided to rush her, but she faked her pose as true as she could.

The pile of laundry was almost a campfire now, and it was starting to spread horizontally, toward her vanity.

Jack recovered from his hit to the groin and poised himself to pounce. Grady lowered his hand near his crotch and mimed a masturbatory motion, then turned and leaped through the window in a single bound, taking a few more loose shards of glass with him. Kat heard the sound of his body hitting the transformer outside, then the ground, followed by a deep grunt of manly pain.

Kat ran to the window, peered out. Grady was gone.

But the disaster was not over yet. Jack dashed into the bathroom. The water ran for a few seconds, then he returned with a soaked bath towel. He spread it as wide as the wet fabric would allow and dropped it atop the rising flame. It landed with a splat and doused the fire, a tight pink prophylactic hugging a mound of diseased black.

Jack turned to Kat, breathing heavily. He could barely get the words out. "Holy . . . holy shit, are you okay?" he asked. "Kat?"

All Kat could think was: at least she wouldn't have to wash that huge pile of laundry anymore.

Jack squatted down and picked up his glasses. He put them on. One of the lenses was almost completely broken out, while the other miraculously seemed untouched.

"So after all this is over," Jack said, "you wanna help me pick out a new pair?"

Kat did not acknowledge his attempt to deflect through humor. Her hands went limp. She dropped the knives, smiled weakly, and leaned her head against Jack's shoulder.

"Okay," Jack continued. "It's time to make our move. We can't wait. I'm calling Wade and the others. You ready?"

Kat shrugged. "Ready as I'll never be."

CHAPTER TWENTY

ALMOST MIDNIGHT. All Hallows Eve long gone, *Dia de los Inocentes* nearing its end, and *Dia de los Muertos* mere moments away. The cycle would soon be complete. Grady was fed up with the events of the day, even more than the average day. He had set out on a mission to kill immediately following his transformation. No real rhyme or reason to it. Did there need to be a reason, though, when he just plain enjoyed soaking his hands in a person's insides? It was the little things in life that pleased him. Appendixes, spleens, rectums. He didn't ask for much.

But there was a problem nevertheless. His killing spree had failed miserably. He was not used to failure. He always got the girl. He was financially in the black. His team always won. Everything had been going so well, all up until tonight in Van Nuys when his luck went right down the shitter. Kat Dyer should have been easy pickings, and she would have been had she been alone. He would have peeled her scabs off individually, slowly like day-old Band-Aids, the kind that refused to let go of hair and flesh. No challenge at all. Instead she had ended up being a literal pain in the ass. And he was still in shock that Jack Lantin, who he had always thought amounted to nothing more than a hipster scarecrow, was able to best him. The night certainly hadn't started off very well.

But the night was far from over. Now he believed his luck was about to turn around. It certainly couldn't get worse.

He stood before the glass doors of Cosmo's Custom Costumes. There were no streetlights nearby, seemingly no lights on within the store. He was surrounded by the thick, dark syrup of night. He knew this spot was where the true transformative power lay. This place, or rather some force seething within its walls, was why he was reborn. It had to be. There was no other logical option. He had already believed it, then overhead Kat, Jack, and Hannah talking about it earlier, which somehow confirmed it. He wanted to harness the power, push it deeper, evolve into something far greater than he had already become. Why stop at taking over Hollywood when he could have San Francisco, Belize City, Reykjavik, Florence, Des Moines?

He placed the palm of his hand against the cool glass. The heat from his flesh caused it to steam an outline, making it look like Mickey Mouse had paid a visit. The steam extended further beyond his rough fingers, highlighted the various fingerprints and splashes of dirt that had been decorating the glass for days, weeks, months.

His reflection should have shocked him, but he already knew his face would be a raw, pink mess. Slight patches of hair matted to the top of his head. Eyebrows half gone. He would never be able to claim to be a pretty boy again. It didn't matter anymore. Power would be his new pretty.

It was after hours. Long after. No one would be here at the costume shop, and if they were they would surely be sorry they were burning the midnight oil. On some level, he hoped there would be someone here, someone cleaning up the maddening mess left in the wake of post-Halloween 50 percent off sales, someone he could tie up tightly and torment and learn all the trade secrets from. He wanted to shake the hidden hand that had been played behind the curtain, meet the mastermind behind this game.

There was a pumpkin on the ground, placed just to the side of the door, a rudimentary grinning face painted on its skin. The bastards couldn't even be bothered to carve a proper Jack-o'-lantern. It was heavily bruised, already showing the early signs of rot. Grady crouched and smashed his fist into it. It only took two tries before it caved in. When he removed his hand it was covered in pulp. Grady smirked as he slopped it back and forth between both hands. The motion relaxed him. Meat was meat, and guts were guts.

The scent of pumpkin brought him back to an incident that happened three Halloweens ago, when he was still Lucas and naturally assumed he always would be Lucas. He and some friends were driving down Sunset, looking for trouble, as any self-respecting young American male should be doing on Halloween night. Bryce Patterson was driving, Chase Mann was riding shotgun, and Lucas was directly behind Chase. What really irked Grady now was that he couldn't remember who else was in the back seat with him. With Lucas. He could remember every other distinct detail about that night like it happened five minutes ago, but couldn't recall who was sitting right next to him, the person who he'd likely had the most conversation with that night. He tried to find answers from Lucas, but Lucas wasn't responding.

They were screwing around in Silver Lake earlier in the evening, looking for shit to wreck, people to throw firecrackers at, pumpkins to smash. Eventually they came across a house with a huge pumpkin sitting on the porch. The pumpkin was the size of a pregnant woman's belly, if she was set to have sextuplets. Lucas yelled at Bryce to pull over because he had to have this orange behemoth. He knew it would cause a bigger mess than anything else they'd find. Guts a' plenty just waiting to explode. It was perfect.

They took their time, cruised over to Sunset. All kinds of douchebags in ironic costumes and stupid sluts dressed like slutty versions of something decidedly non-slutty. Bo-ring. Grady wondered what had happened to dressing as something terrifying. The world didn't need any more costumes based on puns. People needed to get back to their roots. Stay scary. Otherwise, what was the point? At least he was still carrying the torch. He hadn't lost his self-respect.

They passed by a club where a bunch of hipster morons were hanging out in the front, and none of them were even wearing a costume. Even worse than slutty or funny. Just nothing. NO effort. Too cool for school. Lucas was dressed as a demonic priest that night. Black robe complete with giant upside-down cross hanging from his neck to trigger anyone who cared. Simple, yet effective.

Lucas told Bryce to spin back around. This was the place that was going to get bombed. But they had to time it perfectly, make sure the stoplight ahead of them was just about to turn green, that they'd be able to peel out before anyone had the chance to read the license plate. It was looking even better when they came around again because people were spilling out toward the curb, just gabbing away. Lucas saw this chick in a short dress that almost showed her snatch and knew she was the one. He'd smash the ginormous pumpkin right behind her, it'd burst, and her cute little outfit (and her night) would be absolutely ruined. Seemed foolproof.

However, sometimes what a person thinks will go perfectly well goes very, very wrong. Or depending on one's point of view, even more perfectly than it could have been had it gone correctly.

Bryce drove at a normal pace so as not to seem suspicious, which meant Lucas's timing had to be spot on. And it was. Couldn't have been better if he'd had the chance to practice six dozen times. He had varsity basketball to thank for those much-needed skills.

He leaned half his body out the window, clutching the huge pumpkin in both hands. When the time came to throw it, he put in as much strength as he could muster and slammed it to the ground.

But it didn't break. Didn't smash. Didn't even crack.

Instead, the next few seconds seemed to play out in slow motion. The pumpkin hit the ground just behind the girl and bounced, flying the few extra inches it needed to crash directly into the girl and knock her over like a spare bowling pin. Lucas glanced back as they drove off and saw the girl kneeling on the ground, clutching the back of her leg. Had to have hurt. Ruined her night. Just not in the way Lucas had planned. Po-tay-to. Po-tah-to.

It felt good to wax nostalgic, to reflect on what had come before, but Lucas's memories were fading fast. Grady was taking over. Soon he would be all that remained.

He kicked the busted pumpkin out of the way, then wiped the pulp on his filthy jumpsuit.

With his bare fist, Grady punched through the glass of the front door. Super-strength—one of the many advantages of being spawned from a slasher film. The crash sounded like utter chaos on the otherwise silent street. Shards pierced his knuckles and his wrist. He didn't care. Glass wedged in his face, glass slicing his hands—there was no difference.

He barely bled. The pain was cleansing. It was true religion. It throbbed like a determined alarm clock deep within his body, screaming at him to wake the fuck up because time was of the essence. However, no alarm sounded off inside Cosmo's, and for this he was thankful. The last thing he needed was to draw more attention to himself.

A lone car puttered along the street past the strip mall that was home to Cosmo's. Grady froze, a mannequin on the wrong side of the window, until he could no longer see the taillights. He twisted the lock on the other side, pulled his arm away from the door, shook off the excess glass, plucked out a few tiny shards attempting to take root in his hand. He stepped across the threshold, knowing he had zero plans to return to the outside world without concrete answers, without a clear set of instructions regarding the dark magic that made him one with Lucas. Made Lucas one with Grady. He was not sure if he was one, the other, or an amalgam of the two anymore, or if it even mattered. It took two to tango.

He decided it didn't matter. It certainly wouldn't once this night was over. This version of himself was just a chrysalis. There were better things to come. Why stop at being a world-famous cinematic serial killer when there were greater glories to be had? He didn't want to punch out and go home from this job until he earned the promotion to Vengeful God.

Broken glass crunched beneath his boots like insect husks. Inside the shop, it would have been pitch black were it not for the faint green light shining just past the front counter, a light beckoning him to the other side of the store. A light illuminating an elongated hallway that could not possibly fit within the confines of this small building.

The hallway was where he needed to go. Whoever it was he sought, they were waiting for him. Somewhere. He was certain. He was prepared for answers to questions he hadn't yet thought up. He drooled at the thought of violence, both before he learned the truth and after, even if he didn't have to resort to it. The more senseless, the better. All life was beneath him. Self-preservation and absolute power were the only things that counted.

He limped across the hard, tiled floor as quietly as he could. He thought he heard faint voices, the cadence of chanting, but he couldn't be sure. The light never seemed to get brighter as he moved closer to the hallway.

Footsteps behind him. He spun around, reaching into his
pockets for something to slice with, but there was nothing. He'd
neglected to secure a weapon after escaping from Kat's apartment.
He cracked his knuckles, ready to use the weapons he was reborn
with.

A man stood in the shadows. Though Grady could not see his
face, the man was unmistakably holding a gun. A gun pointed right
at him.

"Welcomes," the man said. "We've been waiting for you."

Grady loosened his stance. He patted around his waist, realized
he must have lost his knife during the struggle with Jack. His fists,
mighty as they were, were no match for a bullet. He was going to
have to play nice.

"Who the fuck are you?" Grady asked.

The man cackled. "The fuck am I? You, crazed man, have come
to my store. You are meeting Cosmo himself." He tapped at his chest
with his free hand, shot Grady a devilish smile.

"Well, tickle my dick and call it a sweet pickle. Looks like you're
just the guy I need to talk to, then."

"No. Not I. The one you seek is there." He motioned toward the
dim hallway.

"You don't say. That was my next stop."

"It is clear you are strong. Perhaps you are worthy."

"Oh, yeah?" Grady spat a wad of black phlegm on the ground.
Cosmo grimaced. "Not that I don't appreciate the potential
compliment, but worthy of what?"

"Remains to be seen. If you can proving yourself. Only Maa can
judge."

"This 'Maa' guy, he's the one with the power to change me like
this? To make me even stronger?"

"Not 'he.' Maa is woman you won't want to be fucking with."

Grady giggled. "Hee! Oh, we'll see about that. No woman ever
got the best of me. And I'll be fucking with whomever the hell I
please. But . . . since she's the one with the magic, I'm willing to see
what she has to offer. I'm a reasonable man, when I'm in the mood."
He held up his hand to Cosmo, making sure he could see that his
forefinger and middle finger were crossed.

"You go now." Cosmo motioned to the hall again. "There."

Grady made a fist, punched his palm, then switched and did the same with opposite hands. Repeat. Repeat. "Alrighty. Not like I got anything better to do." He turned and headed toward the green light. "Just don't be a total shit and shoot a man in the back, yeah?"

He reached a doorway with no actual door to be found, soon followed by a fork with two pathways to choose from. He heard chanting again. It could have been coming from either side, or neither. Echoes were the mischievous imps of the sonic spectrum.

"So which way do I go?" He turned, slowly, so as not to tempt Cosmo's trigger finger. He turned, only to discover Cosmo was no longer there.

And neither was the open doorway.

What had been empty space mere moments ago was now sealed off. And it was no illusion. He placed his palm against it. It was cold, hard stone.

"Well, I'll be damned. This is one freaky fun house."

He had to move forward, decide which fork to take. He considered an eeny, meenie, miny, moe, but decided against it. He'd read somewhere that the song had racist origins, but ultimately wasn't bothered by that possibility. There was a deeper issue he was having difficulty confronting. When using this rhyme in childhood, he had never been able to figure out if the "it" was actually "it" or "not it." Too confusing, not worth the trouble. He cursed and chose the left-hand path simply because he was a southpaw.

The dim green light never intensified. The hall never stopped being a hall. In a rare existential moment, Grady wondered if, in fact, a hall could actually cease to be a hall at some point. And, if so, what would it then become?

He couldn't find a room, though it only seemed reasonable that he should have come across one by now. A storage space, a restroom, a kitchenette—something. After all, what would be the purpose of such a long hall leading to what was ostensibly nowhere? Seemed like a waste of space.

He took a few more steps, just for good measure, then stopped and decided to turn around. This path was a waste of time. Dammit, he knew he should have gone right.

After heading back in the opposite direction for a few minutes, he decided someone was playing a prank on him. There was no way he shouldn't have reached the fork again by now. Had he somehow gotten turned around in the dull light that appeared to have no tangible source? Even if that were the case, he still should have reached some sort of endpoint by now. A wall, a back door, something. The building itself did not extend this far. He supposed it was possible he might be on a downward slope, but it would have to have been so gradual that it wouldn't have made a significant difference in square footage anyway.

But, he realized, if a wall could appear out of thin air, it stood to reason that a hallway could go on forever. The rules had changed upon entering Cosmo's Custom Costumes.

Now he was just getting pissed.

He felt along the wall, just knowing he would eventually have to come across a hidden door, but also realizing that door might be on the other wall, that he'd have to go back the opposite direction once (*if*) he arrived at the end of the hall. Back and forth, back and forth. He had already lost track of time, but it was also as if time did not exist in this narrow hall.

Something dark, moist, and shiny skittered across the floor. Difficult to see, but definitely an insect, almost certainly a cockroach. Grady was happy to see something alive in this labyrinth, even something so loathsome, then remembered the average cockroach could survive conditions that would eradicate most other life.

The cockroach paused near the slight curve where the floor met the wall, then pressed up against the wall and disappeared. This was the moment of truth. There had to be some way out of this hell, even if it was just a crack that needed to be chipped away at. His hand still pressed against the wall, Grady picked up his pace and jogged a few steps to where the roach had vanished.

His fingers brushed across an abnormality in the stone wall. He paused, then felt it again. Up and down. It seemed to be a straight line that went from nearly ceiling to floor, then shot across for three feet or so. A door. Had to be. But a door with seemingly no traditional means of opening. He wedged his fingers as far into the crack as he could and tried to make it budge. He pulled back quickly, slipped, and broke off a huge chunk of fingernail. It throbbed and bled, but it did not stop him from carrying on. In fact, he almost begged for more pain. The pain grounded him, reminded him he was not trapped in a dream. He attempted to open the door again. And again. After turning his fingertips into something resembling ground beef, he finally felt the doorway shift, an inch at most.

He paused, reconsidered. What if the roach had been heading home to its filthy family and, on the other side, a sea of tiny foul beasts awaited him? Stacked from floor to ceiling in a quivering mass, their weight prepared to crush him, enter every orifice, and swallow him whole. He was otherwise out of options. If he was to become fodder for vermin, then so be it. Better than to be lost in limbo forever. He grunted and pulled and put all of his remaining strength into the feat of pulling the concrete door open.

And he succeeded! It was so glorious he almost cheered. The door swung open slowly, but it opened wide enough for him to slip through. More dim light on the other side, just like before, but perhaps a slightly different shade of green. Or perhaps his eyes were playing tricks on him. The same cold, barren concrete walls formed the hall. He looked left and right, couldn't decide which would be the smarter path to take, or if either would even be an improvement over his current predicament. He turned back to the wall and realized he had no choice but to make a choice.

The door was gone.

It wasn't the kind of thing a man got used to.

But there was another door, on the opposite side of the new hall. The same shape and size as the one he had just opened. He could barely see some sort of light outlining this new entrance.

This new door was no easier to open than the first, but at least his fingers were numb now. What awaited him on the opposite side was not what he expected.

A seemingly unending sea of flames. Blue that bled into white. Heat that surged into a frostbitten wonder. The tips of the flames whipped toward him like flirty fingers. He felt the tingle of fluctuating temperatures. It was soothing. It was honest.

But he was not seduced by the call of these tongues.

Not yet. Not completely.

He shut the door, but left it open. Just a crack. Just a crack in case he decided to return this way to end it. Just in case he was too weak to pry it back open.

Assuming he'd be able to find it again.

He pressed his fingers to his shut eyes, applying so much pressure that he was in danger of gouging them out. He finally gave up on his silence and howled in frustration, then smashed his fist against the wall. The impact broke at least a few bones, turned his knuckles to pulp, but he didn't care.

He pressed forward, into the dim green hell.

For moments or forever, he couldn't tell. It could have been either.

Eventually, the green bled into a reddish hue. More chanting. Not on either side of the wall, but seemingly inside the walls. Perhaps it was the walls themselves. Grady wasn't ruling that possibility out.

There was a room at the end of the hall. A room with no door. From inside bled a deep red light like something out of Amsterdam.

He wasn't sure how long it took to reach the room, but reach it he did. When he passed through the doorway, it felt like his head was in a vacuum. He went temporarily deaf.

A woman hovered among the crimson shadows. Something that should have been a woman but was more accurately birthed from the bowels of hell. No. Not hell. This was a beast birthed from tales other than those he had learned in Sunday school.

A young, rugged man with a bald head and goatee and a plump younger woman, both naked, kneeled before the creature. They suckled at her bare, wrinkled feet, scratched at her thighs.

She squeezed her own breasts. A thick, dark liquid spewed out, bathing the two devotees.

When her teats went dry, the beast's eyes met Grady's gaze. Her mouth formed into something resembling a smile. Grady felt his crotch go damp.

It was the first time in Grady Sullivan's short stint in the physical world that a raw scream left his lips.

And it was also the last.

CHAPTER TWENTY-ONE

I T WAS NEARLY three in the morning. Pure black blanketed the sky, save a stray star or two. In a deserted parking lot, two buildings down from Cosmo's Custom Costumes, Jack stood poised like a reluctant drill sergeant. Kat hovered near Jack's side, barely able to stay awake. She'd barely had a moment's rest since waking up this morning. And losing pieces of herself along the way sure as hell didn't give her additional strength. First the nipple, then some of her hair fell out before they left to pick up Jonah. One of her fingertips had fallen off on the drive over. She'd swallowed a tooth, spat out another.

Time was of the essence. She could feel herself fading.

Their team was assembled. A united team seeking a solution, or unforgiving vengeance—whichever got them what they wanted quicker. Not everyone they'd contacted had been willing or able to participate, but at least they had numbers now.

Jack walked down the loosely formed line of freakish amateur fighters. Kat shambled behind him, barely able to keep up. She gave up after a few steps. Jack seemed ready to inspire them, but there was no pep talk prepared. He returned to the beginning of the line without a peep. What could be said to a group of people they mostly knew only in passing, well aware there was a chance they were sending them to their deaths? *Nice meeting you all, hope you make it out in one piece? We don't know if this is going to work, but we don't have any better ideas? Good luck!*

No. Meaningless words would not suffice. Earlier Jack had told Kat they were redshirts, all of them, and that was the simple truth of the matter. She wasn't sure what he'd meant, but agreed to avoid seeming dense.

But it wouldn't come down to war. The threat of violence would be enough. These people in the costume shop had done horrible things to them, but Kat felt they could still be reasoned with. And Jack agreed. Almost everyone in their group was wealthy to some degree. Everyone but Kat, really. At the very least they had something to exchange.

Jack pulled her aside. "I don't want you going in there," he said, handing her the keys to the Volvo. "You're too weak. Just lean back and rest. Once we get everything sorted out I'll come back and get you."

"K." She was lying. Sure, she would wait in the car just as he had asked. But only temporarily. She couldn't let him face the situation alone. Despite being barely able to move or even speak without experiencing discomfort, she had given up on being a victim. She was owning her fate but not accepting it as final. She was prepared to take her life back.

"Goddammit," Jack said, looking at his watch. "Where the hell are Wade and Edgar? They should have been here by now. We can't wait for them much longer."

"They'll come. They won't let us down."

"Alright, uh, team," Jack said. He walked the short line again, this time slowly enough for Kat to keep up. "We know someone's in there. I peeked in the side window and I can confirm there's at least one employee working, but we don't know how many are actually there, so we need to be careful."

First in line was Lanie Gallagher. Kat had been in countless classes with her over the years, yet barely knew more about her than her name. Lanie was armed with a katana blade, dressed like a flirtatious schoolgirl, her hair bright turquoise, her eyes unnaturally large. She was animated, two-dimensional, thin as rice paper, from Toontown by way of Tokyo.

"Are you ready to take the enemy down?" Jack asked.

"Hai!" Lanie replied. She struck a pose straight out of Cosplay 101. Kat supposed that was a suitable response. She only hoped

Lanie's blade, which was thinner than her body, could do some damage if need be.

Next was Sidney Gates. Kat had regretfully made out with him once at a party back in high school, and it was never spoken of again. Now he was half-man/half-robot. An amalgam of flesh and steel. He stood at attention, not because he was a natural soldier, but because his reconstructed body only allowed for so much movement. He was a man made solely of metal when all they needed was one who possessed mettle.

"Can those fists of yours crack some skulls?" Jack asked. He slapped Sidney's squared shoulder.

Sidney's head sparked. A noise like a broken kazoo came from somewhere within his boxy torso. "Does. Not. Compute."

Jack glanced sideways at Kat. He appeared to be wavering between concerned and confident.

The next arguable warrior was Bryce Patterson. Part of Lucas Lane's Young Republican/FBLA crew. Once staunchly committed to a wardrobe full of preppy pastel shorts and sweaters to drape around his shoulders, now adorned with a straw sombrero, a wool poncho, a thick, black mustache, and unnaturally brown skin. He was munching on a churro. With each bite, some of the cinnamon sugar remained on his mustache.

"Hmm," Jack said, "Well I don't know if you can fight, but at least you showed up. That counts for something I suppose."

"*Órale,*" Bryce replied.

"You know," Kat said, her voice a raspy whisper, "your costume is culturally insensitive."

Bryce squinted and stared her down. He beat at his chest with the tips of his fingers. "*Ey, chica, estos son mi gente ahora.*"

Kat looked at Jack and coughed. Neither of them could conceal their worry any longer. Beggars, choosers, could they coexist in such desperate times? Jack shrugged and moved on to the next volunteer.

This was their lynchpin. Their sure thing. Freddie Wright. An acquaintance of Jack's. A linebacker's build that blended into the gigantic head of a Tyrannosaurus Rex. His teeth were so jagged and sharp they were risky to look at for fear of losing an eye.

"Ready, Freddie?" Kat cringed immediately after the words left Jack's lips. No one else seemed to notice, even Jack.

Freddie roared and hissed and shrieked, ready to disembowel his enemies and decorate the walls with their innards. He had still been able to form simple words when Jack had spoken to him just over an hour ago, but not anymore. At least he seemed to still be able to understand. His long scaly tail whipped from behind, beating at the asphalt, breaking apart small pieces. Thankfully the transformation had not affected his arms. They were concrete slabs hidden beneath veiny flesh. They could do some damage. With Freddie on their side they could win. Kat hoped they at least stood a chance. Who knew what they were about to face?

A girl named Kelly stood next to the dinosaur man. Kat couldn't remember her last name, and it was bothering her to an irrational degree. A cliché bombshell. Long, blonde hair. Legs for days and red heels that added at least a few extra hours to that time frame. Breasts that seemed to move of their own volition. She wore a nurse's uniform that was far too naughty for any legitimate medical activity. Not the most appropriate attire for anything save the bedroom. She smacked on a giant wad of grape bubble gum, which made her seem more like an old mare than a young man's fantasy. Kat noticed that Jack had difficulty taking his eyes off her. He was driving 55 on the off-ramp to Boner City. Even in the face of imminent danger, Jack was still a slave to his hormones.

"I don't get it," Kat said. "You look exactly the same as you did at the party. What gives?"

Kelly looked down at her outfit, as if she forgot what she was wearing. "Oh, this? I didn't get my costume here. I'm just here for moral support."

"Fair enough," Kat said. "Thanks?"

Kelly winked and leaned slightly closer to Kat, but not too close. She dropped her voice to a whisper. "Freddie and I hooked up last night at Hannah's. I'm, uh . . . really hoping for the chance to do that again, but . . . not like *this*, you know?"

Kat nodded. To turn back the clock—this was what they all wished for. Unfortunately, for a few of them, a reset button would be of no help.

Last in line was Jonah. Dressed in his normal clothes, no longer looking like a gladiator but ready to play the role with sheer conviction, his bulging muscles ready to split the seams of his shirt and jeans.

Jack bumped fists with Jonah. It was an honest gesture. It meant something. They were brothers now. Brothers in war. They nodded at each other in silence.

Kat set her hand atop Jonah's. She stared deeply into his stoic face. He did not recoil from her scabrous grip.

"For Hannah," she said.

Jonah bit his lip. "For Hannah."

CHAPTER TWENTY-TWO

"**T**HE CRAZED ONE, he is surely dead by now," Cosmo said, smirking with certainty. "Maa will have taken him deep below. She will be growing strong from his essence. He will be bothering us no more."

Mahboob tapped his fingers nervously against his lips. "Yes. I have heard his screaming. Very loud. Far too much wild in his cards. You are lucky he was not knowing about your gun. A prop, Cosmo. I cannot believe it. You are not brave. You are a stupid, stupid man."

"A fine prop. Almost perfect replica."

"If you say so."

"We only carry the very best here."

"Do not treat me like a customer."

"And I am *not* stupid, Mahboob."

Mahboob chose to ignore his brother and his tedious remarks. "But there is other problem. If one knows, others could be knowing." It was now technically Monday, the only day of the week Cosmo's Custom Costumes was closed to the public, but that didn't mean they got the day off. They had come in promptly at ten minutes before midnight to take inventory and prepare for the Christmas party rentals that customers would start to order in the next few weeks. An abundance of sexy Santa girls and seductive elves, a few two-person reindeer get-ups. December wasn't as lucrative a month as October, but it was far from the slowest season. Though his family did not celebrate the birth of Jesus Christ, they were happy to celebrate the money brought to their business from the holiday's secular elements. They even carried a few outfits that traditionalists would have found sacrilegious.

They hadn't expected to encounter an intruder during inventory. But at least the problem had been taken care of quickly and relatively quietly.

Mahboob grabbed a sticky note, scribbled CALL WINDOW REPAIRMAN ON THE TUESADAY, and slapped it to the side of the register. "I knew this would be happening. Did I not say this yesterday? In a matter of time, this would be happening."

"Mahboob, you are too much the worrywart." Cosmo grasped Mahboob's shoulder and squeezed it. Something inside Mahboob's body creaked. A muscle, a tendon, a bone, he could not be certain. "Come! We are getting behind. Let us finish the job, then go speaking with Maa about others who could be coming, and I cook you some lunch later. Are you wanting aloo gobi, chana masala, some—"

"We no telling Maa! We find way to fix this mess ourselves."

"We will need the shishyas."

"Fine! Yes!"

"You rang?" Blue Fox said. He and Pink Kitty stood near the fitting rooms. Mahboob had no idea how long they had been there. He was ashamed that he had allowed them to see him in such an angry state. They would lose respect for him, if they even had any in the first place. He took a deep breath, attempted to regain his composure.

"How nice of you to finally be showing up, Pink Kitty," Cosmo said. He shifted his attention to Blue Fox. "How are the numbers in the back?"

"Yeah, yeah everything's solid," Blue Fox said. He stroked his goatee with cocky delight. "You really don't need to call us by our codenames anymore, you know."

"Yes," Cosmo said. "I am knowing."

"It's getting kind of ol—"

"Save it," Pink Kitty said. "We've got an idea."

"And since when we pay you to have ideas?" Mahboob asked. "When are you having opportunities to be speaking of ideas? This is working time."

Pink Kitty just stared at Mahboob, unimpressed. "There's this thing called 'lunch break.' I know it might be a foreign concept to you, but it's a great time to gather your thoughts. Come up with *ideas*."

It infuriated Mahboob that Pink Kitty was not intimidated in the slightest. How dare she undermine his authority? As her supervisor, as a man. This was a job, something to be cherished, not something to gamble with.

"And to be honest," she continued, "I'm surprised this wasn't on the agenda from day one."

"Yes? Go on," Cosmo said. He scanned one more row of fake fingernails and set down his barcode scanner.

"It's pretty simple, really," Pink Kitty said. Her cheeks were so puffy it looked like she had suffered a horrible series of bee stings. "Moolah."

"What is cow noise having to do with this?" Mahboob asked.

Cosmo backhanded Mahboob on his shoulder. "Idiot brother! She means money! Do you not know nothing?"

Blue Fox pointed at Cosmo. "Bingo. These little shits have got plenty of it. And so do their parents. Holy fucking hell, you should have seen the house I went to. That crazy killer guy who came down below tonight? I saw him there. He was one of mine."

"What is your proposal?" Cosmo asked.

"We pick a price and tell 'em as soon as they give us the dough we'll switch 'em back to normal. Done and done. But not until they pay up. Everybody's happy."

"A fine trick."

"Plus," Pink Kitty said. "We've technically already done much worse than extortion. At this point the ones who are still alive will just be happy to think they're getting out relatively unscathed. This should be a piece o' cake. Easy fucking money."

Mahboob nodded silently. There was worth in what the shishyas were suggesting. It was a smart plan. And he felt like a complete fool for not thinking of it first. They had punished the rich for being who they were but had not thought to take away their actual riches. With enough money put away, he could finally afford to leave California, escape the grip of his mother and brother. He yearned for freedom. Freedom at any cost. Where he went, it did not matter.

However, he knew Maa would not support this plan. She was staunchly against materialism. Owning anything more than the essentials was at the top of her list of wrongs. Her goal had been to show the wealthy how little their wealth mattered. She wanted none of it for herself.

Or for her sons.

This plan would have to remain a secret, but he wondered how long Cosmo could keep his mouth shut. His brother suckled much too closely to Maa's teat, but did his loyalty outweigh his greed?

"Yes," Mahboob said. "I am liking how you are thinking. But how we can find them?" He grabbed a piece of cardboard, some duct tape, then headed toward the front door.

Cosmo walked behind the counter, dug around with determination. He lifted some papers above his head. "Order forms, *bevakooph*," he said. "We having their phone numbers. Let us finish our day of scanning, then we will act. We will catch them by surprise."

It would take time, but Mahboob knew they could sort this out civilly, that the money that left the hands of their victims would not be missed.

He opened the door, tried to determine the best placement for the cardboard. "Yes, you are right. First things first."

Mahboob heard a crunch, then felt cold, sharp steel against his throat.

"Don't fucking move."

CHAPTER TWENTY-THREE

THE MISFIT ARMY marched through the door single file, squeezing behind Jack and his hostage.

"Please," the hostage said. "I am not hurting you."

"Shut up," Jack said. At least the guy had the sense to hold still, but he sure as hell didn't want to listen to any pleading.

The other employees temporarily froze in their spots, perhaps unsure if this were an elaborate prank being pulled at their expense.

"Oh, fucking hell," the bald man with the goatee said. "It's them."

Jack pushed his hostage closer to the center of the store, near the giant English walnut tree. He put his back to the tree so no one would have the chance to sneak up behind him. The rest of his group split up, surrounding the three remaining employees.

The man behind the counter ducked. When he emerged, his hands were wrapped tight around a wooden baseball bat. There was no fear in his eyes.

"Cosmo!" the hostage yelled. "What you doing?"

So that's the infamous Cosmo, Jack thought. *He knows what's going on. He knows why we're here. All of these assholes do.*

Cosmo came out from behind the counter, wielding his bat like a professional player who was fed up with the umpire. "I be helping you, Mahboob. This is no replica!"

Any other day, the name of his hostage would have made him

snicker. He'd have to make sure to have a good laugh with Kat about the name later on. Once this was all over.

"You'd better stay right where you are," Jack said. He forced his best tough guy voice. "I don't want to cut this guy's throat, but I will."

Cosmo halted. The rest of Jack's group stood silent, awaiting any sort of signal that might tell them what to do. But Jack wasn't even sure what he was doing. In the midst of the day's mad events, he hadn't taken the time to think through what they were doing. Under normal circumstances he wouldn't even be holding a hunting knife. He was barely able to spread peanut butter on bread without making a mess. But here he was, wielding a dangerous weapon that had been left behind by Lucas Lane, or whatever Lucas had become. Whatever these people had turned him into.

"What are you wanting?" Cosmo asked, still clutching the bat tight.

"My friends here," Jack said, trying to remain cool and calm, "they just want their lives back. We know someone here at your shop was involved. Maybe it was you. Maybe it was all of you. I don't know and I don't fucking care. Just change them back, and we'll go for now. No one has to get hurt. No one else, I mean. But we'll be back again later. There are others."

"Pink Kitty," Mahboob said, turning to the round woman, then the bald man with the goatee. "Blue Fox. Telling him the deal now."

Blue Fox. Jack hadn't forgotten about him. He'd tried to find him at the party after comforting Kat, to no avail. He glared at baldy. Blue Fucking Fox.

"You," Jack said.

Blue Fox looked at the woman who was presumably Pink Kitty, then behind him, then back at Jack. "Who, me?"

"It was you. You're the fucking asshole who assaulted Kat."

Blue Fox chuckled, cracked his knuckles. "Oh . . . *yeah*. The chick in the cabana. The one with the freaky costume. Almost had her. So close yet so far. How's she doin', by the way? She fall apart yet?"

Jack had to control his rage. Now was not the time for wiping the smile off this guy's face. Now was the time to negotiate, to save his friends. And those who were not exactly his friends but still didn't deserve the horrors they had been subjected to.

"Telling him!" Mahboob yelled. "Please now."

"Okay," Blue Fox said. "Sure, why not?"

"You tell them nothing!" Cosmo said.

Blue Fox flipped Cosmo the bird. "Sit and spin, man. I'm sick of your attitude and this shitty job. I busted my ass for your Hindu magic bullshit, and what the fuck am I getting out of it? Nada. Zilch. I want a solid payday for once."

"This is not a good way to ask for raise."

"Telling him!" Mahboob yelled again.

Blue Fox turned back to Jack. "Sorry to tell you, bro. Your pals earned a one-way ticket only."

"No," Mahboob said. "Please be quiet again!"

Blue Fox gleeked in Mahboob's direction. The spittle landed less than an inch from Jack's feet.

"What?" Jack said. "What the fuck do you mean?"

"Gimme a break man. Are you dense? Your friends are screwed six ways from Sunday. There ain't no turning 'em back. The potion these jokers had us spread around, there's no fuckin' antidote or whatever. And before you say anything, no I'm not bluffing."

Jack's heart sank. The tension made him shake. Everyone on his team shifted uncomfortably. This wasn't going well. What was he going to tell Kat? How could he face her again and say he was wrong—that he couldn't save her after all? There had to be another way.

Everything from that point on happened so quickly that Jack could barely register it. Lanie released a painful wail and bounced into the air, swiping a sword at every light bulb she could find, destroying them with perfect aim. The inside of the store now nearly matched the darkness outside. Freddie roared and charged forward, knocking into Jack with his gargantuan dinosaur head, then lumbering straight toward Cosmo. Jack dropped his knife, and Mahboob squirmed out of his grip and ran toward the counter.

Cosmo swung the bat at Freddie's massive form, but the young man-turned-T. Rex was too quick. Freddie opened his terrible maw and caught the bat between his thick, sharp teeth. Splinters of wood fell to the ground. Cosmo refused to let go. He tugged on the bat as hard as he could, but it did not budge. Thick, slimy saliva dripped from Freddie's mouth, coating Cosmo's hair like styling gel. Cosmo released one hand, formed it into a fist, and beat it against the side of Freddie's head, but his efforts were futile. Freddie crushed the bat between his teeth and shrieked, his rancid breath spreading across the store.

Cosmo turned to run. Had he hesitated just a few seconds less he might have had a chance to escape. But Freddie made his move. He chomped down on Cosmo's head and tore it from his neck in a single motion. Strands of flesh flapped about, blood ejaculated on Freddie's face and anything else within range, and Cosmo's headless body continued to take a few steps before finally collapsing. Freddie crunched down on Cosmo's skull, then belched.

Jack cringed. He looked into Freddie's reptilian eyes. There appeared to be no humanity left. Controlling him was likely off the table at this point.

Mahboob stared at what was left of Cosmo, his mouth like the entrance to a funhouse.

Jack sprinted toward the front counter. He had hoped it wouldn't come to this, but Freddie had taken them to the point of no return. The violence had begun, and so this confrontation would have to end in violence. No apologies. With Freddie leading the way, there would soon be no one left to apologize to anyway.

But there was one problem, and it was a significant one: Freddie exploded. There was no other way to explain it. One minute he was there, the next he no longer existed, aside from the gore Jack was now covered in.

"Maa!" Mahboob yelled. "You having gotten him!"

Jack wiped some indeterminate goop from his eyes and saw a woman standing—no, *floating* in front of the massive English walnut tree.

The mother. *Maa.*

Smoke drifted from her fingers. It made no logical sense, but there it was. A robe hung loosely on her emaciated body. It was open, exposing a nude, pink, shriveled husk beneath. A body so ancient it would require carbon to determine her age. Hair in places where it shouldn't have been, breasts that hung to her navel, a dark vulva that pulsated as if speaking. Snakelike arms, a mouth full of rotten yet still-sharp teeth. Perhaps most unsettling: a third eye at the center of her brow.

Though she grinned widely, her eyes looked tired. She glanced quickly at Jack, floated down to the ground, and limped toward the fitting rooms.

Whatever power she wielded, using it must have made her weak.

He signaled to Jonah, pointed toward Maa. Jonah nodded, gave Jack a thumbs up.

She would have to be dealt with later.

———— ♦ ————

Lanie launched toward Pink Kitty, light as a sheet of paper, and just as thin. She made noises that sounded closer to a porno sound bite than a battle cry. Pink Kitty threw a punch at her and missed, giving Lanie the chance to slice her with her katana. It made a thin cut across Pink Kitty's cheek, enough to spray blood yet not enough to give her pause.

Pink Kitty screamed with rage, stared unflinchingly at Lanie. She took a chance and looked at the floor, hoping to find a weapon, but Lanie took advantage of this briefly broken concentration. Within seconds she was in mid-air, her flying kick connecting with Pink Kitty's buxom breasts and knocking her into a rack of faux fur coats and flapper dresses.

Lanie contorted her two-dimensional body into an exaggerated pose, ready to strike.

Pink Kitty recovered quickly from the fall, stood and grabbed a dress from the rack, and wrapped it around the hangar. She dug into her pocket and pulled a lighter free, flicked it and lit it on the first try, then set the flame underneath the dress. The rayon dress burned fast and bright.

Lanie turned to run, but she was not quick enough. Pink Kitty swung the burning dress and it connected with Lanie's film-thin body, almost wrapping around it like a flaming anaconda. She quickly became one with the flame. Barely a few seconds of screaming before nothing was left of her but ash. Pink Kitty stomped out the remaining embers.

She breathed heavily, cracked her knuckles, ready to find her next opponent. Before she could take a step, two steel hands wrapped around her face, the fingers digging into her eyes. She released a few hog-like screams, struggled but failed to pry the fingers away as they pushed deep down. Jellied blood and other assorted fluids oozed from her sockets. She went limp, then one of the hands pulled away and clasped at her throat, crushing it just enough to make the difference between life and death.

Pink Kitty's body dropped to the floor. Sidney the robot stood his ground, victorious, his shiny body soaked in red.

"I'm. Sorry," he said. "But. You. Killed. My. Friend."

———————— ◆ ————————

Jack frantically tried to find the hunting knife in the darkness. He couldn't get his bearings among the chaos, couldn't figure out where he'd even dropped it in the first place. It was too dark.

He stopped, looked in the direction of the front door. Someone was standing there.

Kat.

She was doing her best to steer clear of the war, leaning against a life-sized facsimile of a phone booth. She was weak. In shock. Rotting faster. Her tired bones could barely support her enough to stand. She looked worn and defeated, not like the Kat who had been bursting with life just mere days ago. Jack ran to her side.

"Goddammit, why are you in here?" Jack asked. "You were supposed to wait in the car."

Her left eye was now an empty socket. Her bottom lip drooped. Her face was raw, pink meat. "Couldn't. Had to come help."

Jack wasn't able to hold back the disgust he felt inside. It commandeered his face, and he hoped Kat was too far gone to notice. He could barely get his next words out. "Oh fuck, Kat. You're just going to get yourself hurt. More hurt. Are you okay?"

"No. Not even close."

"Just stay here. Don't let them see you. Stay out of the way. Please."

Kat gave him a look that was difficult to read. She nodded. Jack grabbed a small handful of her short hair, just enough to be loving, and lightly kissed the final patch of her forehead that was not covered in oozing sores. It was damp with sweat. "I'll be back."

"Be . . . careful."

He smiled at her. "Of course I will."

It was the only lie he'd ever told her.

"Jack. I just wanted to tell you. I—"

"Shh." Jack put his finger to Kat's lips. "We'll talk after."

"K."

Jack turned just in time to see Blue Fox strangling Bryce to death with his own poncho.

———— ♦ ————

Mahboob crouched behind the register, his back against the glass. He had to do something, but he had no idea what. Cosmo was dead, and Maa was growing weak from using her powers. He was not a fighter, but he was also not ready to die. He had to leave. Now.

Before he had the chance to make a move, he was pulled up to his feet, the back of his shirt caught in someone's fist.

He struggled and squirmed and soon broke free of the grip, but not without tearing away a huge chunk of his shirt. He turned to see a disturbing blend of man and machine, some sort of technology that did not yet exist. His instinct told him to punch, and he did, immediately shattering his fingers on the robot's face. He howled in stupid pain.

"Ouch," the robot said, its voice monotone. "That. Hurt. Why. Do. You. Hit. Sidney." The robot's body vibrated and something resembling a bolt fell from its midsection and clanged when it hit the ground. The robot grabbed Mahboob's arm and squeezed, breaking the bones in one motion. And it didn't let go. Mahboob could feel his arm being pulled out of its socket. The pain was too great to scream, so intense he was on the verge of passing out.

Without warning the robot's head split into a dozen pieces. Oil spurted from its neck. Tendrils of wire flopped back and forth.

Maa crouched behind its steel body, hissing, her forked tongue flapping in the air like a windsock. She lightly shoved the robot's shell, and it collapsed. Her hands sizzled, and Mahboob felt a sensation not unlike mild electric shock.

"Beta," she said. "You must quit being a coward. Fight, fool, fight! We cannot lose. Kali is watching. Always watching."

Mahboob stared at his mother as she floated off, barely able to stay balanced despite defying gravity.

———— ♦ ————

After a few moments of intimate fisticuffs, Jonah kneed Blue Fox below the belt, just shy of his groin but still enough to make him flinch. He quickly recovered and knocked Jonah to the ground, kicking him in his side so many times that his foot sounded like military percussion against his ribcage.

Jonah was dazed but not down for the count. He curled into a ball and rolled a few feet away, giving him the chance to pull out a small folding knife he had stuffed in the side of his sock. He flipped it open. Blue Fox did not notice and attempted another kick, but Jonah grabbed his foot before it could connect. He ripped the knife underneath Blue Fox's leg, across his Achilles tendon. Blue Fox's eyes stretched wide, his mouth gaped open in a silent scream. Blood spurted and sprayed across Jonah's face and chest, and Blue Fox fell. Jonah crouched over him and stabbed him three times in the chest, then another in the stomach for good measure. He wanted to roar in animal rage, but all he could do was whimper. He could barely hold onto the knife. He couldn't believe what he had just done, but it was already too late to take it back. And he didn't have time to sit and wallow in killer's remorse. He left the limp body and marched toward where he had seen the witch go.

———◆———

Mahboob didn't see Jack coming, and Jack took advantage of the situation. He grabbed Mahboob's head and smashed it into the counter, shattering the glass into pieces. Easiest fight he could have hoped for at this point. Mahboob collapsed to the floor. His head was a bloody, sliced up mess. He did not move. Whether he was knocked out cold or dead, Jack could not say, but he had no time to waste and not a care in his body at this point except to protect Kat, so he moved on.

He saw Jonah standing before Maa, ready to face off in front of the tree.

Kelly approached from behind the tree. It was the first time Jack had seen her since the carnage began. Her makeup was smeared from terrified tears, her nurse's uniform torn down the side, from breast to hip. Her body was quivering, but she was still bravely moving forward.

And Kat, mere feet away from both of them, inching closer.

What the hell is she doing? Jack thought. *She was supposed to stay put. Dammit!*

He ran toward them, figuring they might have a chance with three against one. Kat didn't count. She wouldn't be able to hurt a stuffed animal right now. Maa appeared to be their only opponent left at this point, and she was growing weak. They were winning.

They had a real chance. Even though all hope was lost of changing anyone back, they had to make sure they at least came out of this experience with some sort of consolation prize.

After a few quick steps, something latched onto Jack's ankle, tripping him. He toppled into a rack filled with fake blood, vampire teeth, spirit gum, and latex wounds. The hooks these items hung from poked into his body. They did not feel good. There would soon be deep, dark bruises forming, yellow and brown polka dots across his back.

Jack managed to set himself upright, then saw a grinning face staring at him. Teeth painted red, a long, thick goatee dripping with gory filth.

"Not . . . fucking done . . . yet."

———— ◆ ————

Kat could barely think straight. Her body was deteriorating by the moment. Instinct told her to hide and survive, but her commitment to avenging Hannah took precedence. These bastards couldn't get away with the hell they had put her and her friends through.

She tried to lean on her good side as she limped toward the tree. It helped. Slightly. She had always been good at fooling herself.

She was halfway from the front door to the tree now. Jonah was about to face off with the mother. Kelly was acting as backup, standing out of sight. Jonah stood fast, a barely-present knife clutched in his hand, his shirt torn from collar to shoulder. The horrible woman smiled at him in such a way that Kat felt the urge to pee.

"Come on, you dirty freak," Jonah said. "Whattaya got?"

The witch shrieked, and Jonah charged forward with nothing more than bravado and his insignificant weapon.

The evil creature waved her decrepit fingers at Jonah. Kat heard something swish but saw nothing fly through the air. The next thing she saw was half of Jonah's head and torso separating from his body. It didn't make sense to her. One minute he was whole and beautiful, the next she could see the inner workings of his body. She now knew what bone marrow looked like. She couldn't take it anymore. She screamed.

It was a weak and tired scream, but loud enough to be a mistake. It made her entire body quiver and ache, and it also drew attention to her. The mother-demon hadn't noticed her before, but now Kat was in her sights. The slight darkness was not enough to keep her hidden. The woman was visibly weak, but definitely still dangerous, a wounded tiger backed into a corner.

"You," the mother hissed, pointing at Kat. "You think you are special because you are rich? We have shown you just how much your money matters. Worthless filthy whore, you are."

Kat was confused. The fear that filled her transformed into anger. The anger gave her strength. She spat out something thick and slippery. "Seriously? Are you fucking kidding me? I work at a boutique store! I can barely pay my rent!"

The demon glared at her, seemed to size her up. Kat hoped her words worked because they were all she had left to fight with. The woman licked her lips with her long, forked tongue. "It does not matter." Her voice was calm now. Confident. "You will feel no sympathy from me. Money or no money, your pale flesh made you more prosperous than my family could ever have hoped to be. Nothing matters now. Nothing at all." She tried to stand, but could not. She crawled away from the tree.

Kat forced a smile. The fight was almost over.

Except it wasn't.

The mother waved her hand toward the tree. It creaked and shifted. Pieces of the ceiling crashed down. The top of the tree broke through. Its roots tore the floor open. It was moving quickly.

Kat tried to back away, but her strength was gone. And there was nowhere to go.

She tripped over something. A body, a mannequin, she was not sure.

She landed on her back, hit her head. Hard. Her one good eye only saw a stinging flash of light.

The tree fell.

She faintly heard Jack call her name.

And Kat saw no more.

———— ◆ ————

"Kat!" Jack saw Kat fall, saw the tree plummeting, had a moment of respite between punches, and attempted to get up.

"Nope," his opponent said. "You ain't . . . goin' anywhere, man. You're fucking . . . toast." His voice gurgled with thick fluid.

Jack was pulled back to the ground, felt a fist connect to his jaw. For a moment he thought there were birds flying in a halo around his head like in an old cartoon, but soon realized they were real birds fluttering in the open ceiling where the giant tree once was, chirping with anger at the loss of their home. The first dim beams of daylight were creeping in. The sky was beautiful.

He had to get up. He had to get to Kat, make sure she was okay.

She was okay. Of course she was. It was Kat. Tough little Kat.

Blue Fox hovered over Jack. He seemed to have barely any strength left in him. His last punch must have taken the rest of his energy. He attempted to raise his fist again and failed. He spat out a giant globule of phlegm and blood.

"Guess that means you're day-old toast," Jack said. "I win." He spat as well, in an attempt to appear manlier.

Blue Fox looked like he wanted to say something witty, but he didn't have the chance to. Something thin and sharp pierced his eye. He screamed.

A heel. Five inches.

It was Kelly. The Sexy Nurse of Destruction.

She dug the heel deeper into Blue Fox's eye, until it must have penetrated his brain. His body twitched, then did not move again.

Jack took her hand and she helped him up.

"Oh fuck oh fuck oh fuck," Kelly said. "I didn't just do that. Did I do that? Oh, God, what the hell did I just do?"

Jack grabbed her, tried to keep her steady. "You saved my life. Thank y—"

Before Jack could release his grip, Kelly let loose a wail that temporarily made his eardrum go numb. Something weighed down his hand. It took a few seconds for him to register what it was.

Kelly's severed arm.

She couldn't stop shrieking in a wild mix of fear and pain, and Jack couldn't blame her. A waterfall of blood poured from the wound. She wandered off in a daze, falling after a few steps. Jack didn't have time for a tourniquet, which meant she would likely be lost soon. He dropped the arm.

It was just Jack against Maa now. She was temporarily incapacitated, collapsed next to the fallen tree. Whatever powers she had were not infinite. He had to go after her now, while she was recharging.

Still, there was no way he could win. He was also at his weakest. It was almost over. At least it would be over soon. Then he could rest. They all could. Finally.

Most people would claim that a small black pug and a gay man who had never been in a fight in his life would be useless as reinforcements. But that was who showed up in Jack's moment of need. He had never been so happy to see Edgar and Wade in his life. They would fight together and likely die together, but at least he would die knowing he had friends he could count on. That meant something in the grand scheme of things.

"Holy mother of God," Wade said, surveying the warzone that had once been a costume shop. "Oh, this is very, very bad."

"Guys! Hurry! Help me . . . Kat's in trouble. We've gotta get to her, and we've gotta kill this crazy bitch while she's weak!"

"Sorry," Wade said. "We would have been here sooner, but I couldn't find the damned place. When the hell do I ever set foot in Van Nuys?"

"Excuses, excuse," Edgar said. "If I'd been driving . . . ah, fuck it. We're wasting time. Let's do this!" He winked at Jack, kicked his back legs a few times like an angry bull, and ran awkwardly among the debris, toward the roots of the fallen tree, where the weak and wounded old woman lay. She did not see him coming until it was too late. Edgar hopped over a pile of costumes, and Maa waved her hand when he was mere inches away. He clamped his jagged teeth over her fingers and bit as hard as his little mouth would allow. She howled in a mix of surprise and pain. Edgar pulled away and spat out two fingers that had come loose. A thick, grey fluid oozed from her stumps.

"Mmm, mmm," Edgar said. "Finger lickin' good!"

"Now," Jack said. "While she's distracted!" Jack ran toward Maa, stepped over Jonah's half-body, saw the gleam of the fallen gladiator's knife among the carnage, grabbed it, and kept running. Wade followed not far behind.

With her good hand, Maa grabbed Edgar by the ruff of his neck. He struggled but couldn't free himself from her grip. She used her remaining strength to throw him across the room. He flew far, too far to not at least be badly wounded, if not worse. He landed with a thud and a whine, and then went silent.

"Ed! No!" Jack cringed and pressed forward, limping like a determined ghoul, the knife clutched tightly. He exchanged glances with Wade, made a quick motion with his hand. Wade shifted gears, ran off to find Edgar among the debris.

Jack approached Maa. He was afraid that once he was up close and personal with her that she would strike before he had the chance to make his move. He was wrong.

Her old, tired body had betrayed her. Her three eyes looked up at Jack, and it was the first time that he realized the third eye was real, not a costume trick. Of course it was. Costumes were not just costumes anymore. They were a bridge between the old world and the new.

The third eye blinked slowly in unison with the other two. It was almost a mystical moment, the kind that forever altered one's life.

But their lives had already been irrevocably changed. This was just the tiny cherry on top of the shit sundae.

Maa looked pitiful. Demon or no, in this moment she merely looked like an elderly woman who had rolled over in her sleep and fallen from her deathbed. Jack had expected her to let loose one final defiant laugh, or maybe some scripted famous last words. But she just looked old, tired, ready to shuffle to the next world and be reborn into something with its full vitality intact. Her breathing stopped and started again, following anything but a normal pattern.

As he raised the knife, he wondered if what he was doing would be considered self-defense. He decided this wasn't the time to be philosophizing about moral grey areas, and he thrust the knife down into her chest, guessing where her heart was, hoping it was in the same vicinity as a normal person's. Grey blood sprayed all over him from waist to face, barely missing his eyes. He sputtered as it splashed against his lips.

Again, his expectations were not met. He was prepared for some significant event following Maa's death, some inhuman shrieking and howling inferno that stole her body away, removed as if it never existed. Then his friends' lives would be magically restored, and they could face the rest of their long lives together. Happily ever after. But all he was left with was a limp corpse. She could have passed for a decoration in the store that had been knocked over during the battle. He left the knife in her chest. He had no more need for it.

Jack attempted to wipe some of the blood from his shirt, but it was more of a red-grey tie-dye than white now. He briefly considered grabbing something dry from the shop and putting it on once he found Kat, then remembered what they had just been through and decided against it.

He couldn't get up. He had to crawl to the tree, guessing where Kat had been when it fell.

"Jack?" Wade approached from the other side of the store, holding Edgar's limp furry body. Wade was crying. Jack looked away. He couldn't come closing to dealing. Not Edgar. Not his best fucking friend since seventh grade. He hadn't even had the chance to tell Wade about Carey yet. About what Lucas had done. What was he even going to say? This was too much to handle. Too heavy a weight on his soul. Kat had to be okay. Jack couldn't make it without her.

Jack gripped the tree and flung his leg up so he was straddling it, then swung his other leg up and over. A few feet away lay Kat. Jack tried to run toward her and tripped on a branch, tumbling and scraping his arm badly, jamming his pinky finger. He did not feel a thing.

It felt like a slow motion dream as he approached Kat, like his feet were trudging through thick mud. She was resting. She was sleeping. She was fine. Taking a nap, curled up by the tree trunk. Had to be. He couldn't fault her for being exhausted.

Like a cheap drug, the illusion only lasted so long.

Half of her body had been crushed by the tree. Her rotten half. The side of her that was exposed was Kat as he knew her. Kitty Kat. Beautiful, deceptively frail. Her once blonde hair now stained black and red.

"No," he whispered, so quietly it might have actually been inside his head.

Her skull was partly caved in, but she was not dead. Not yet. Soon. Very soon. Short, sharp breaths. Incoherent sounds escaped her mouth, her lips moving desperately, like a fish out of water overdosing on oxygen. One precious blood-filled eye that wandered, seeing nothing. She must have been suffering badly. There was no coming back from this damage.

Wade set Edgar down gently. The body was so tiny, so still. He placed a trembling hand on Jack's shoulder.

Jack held the back of his hand to his mouth. To keep from vomiting, to keep from crying, he was not sure. They had won, and yet they had lost. They had lost everything.

He forced himself to feel nothing, to feel empty.

And it was surprisingly easy.

EPILOGUE

I T MIGHT BE an outdoor shopping center, a business park, a strip mall. It doesn't matter where this moment ends up taking place, but wherever it is, you decide to go there because you live nearby, and it's a convenient place to get in some last-minute shopping. It's somewhere. That's the important part.

It's the week of Halloween, some year, any year, and you've been invited to your very first costume party by some of the most popular people on campus, in the local music scene, in church, whatever. That doesn't matter.

What matters is that you still haven't decided what you want to dress up as. A clown, a sports personality, a vampire—who knows? You've thought about it for months, but just like every other year you procrastinate or you decide your idea isn't clever or attractive enough. And now it's too late to special order a really neat, original costume, so you'll have to choose from something they have in stock. Dems da breaks, kid.

You're hoping for something gender-neutral, so as not to trigger any new friends who might find your choice politically incorrect. You're a sensitive person, and the last thing you want to do is offend anyone. You look to the racks, then at the long line, and you almost decide to come back later. You don't want to spend your whole day here. But you've already driven so far that it'd be a waste of your precious time, not to mention gas, to do this all over again tomorrow.

After perusing your costume options, you find the perfect choice, or what you've convinced yourself out of desperation is the perfect choice. What is it? Again, doesn't matter. As long as it impresses the right people, who cares what the specifics are? Halloween will be your time to shine. Everyone will be looking at you. It will be an unforgettable night. Life will never be the same again.

You're almost to the front of the line now. You can't help but look at the clerk. He's quite a character. You're trying not to stare because that would be rude. He looks tired, like he's seen better days. His fingers on one hand are crooked, his arm slightly deformed, as if it had been broken but never allowed to heal properly. Yet still he does his best to smile because that's an important aspect of working in retail. You know this all too well. You've worked retail ever since your first job in high school. Smiled and swallowed the shit dished out to you until your shifts were over. Suffice to say, you're ready to be done with retail. You can't wait to finish college and move up in the world, start making some real money. Become a real bigwig. In the meantime, you can't help but sympathize with this poor man.

And you decide to trust him because you're a modern person who doesn't like being prejudiced against immigrants and cripples, and he appears to be a combination of the two. And why shouldn't you trust him? He's only the guy who works at the costume shop. He's harmless. He's only trying to make a living in America. He deserves a chance. It's only fair.

One more customer, and then you're there, ready to make your purchase. You can see some accessories behind the counter you're going to have to ask about, the sort of items an opportunist would opt to shoplift were they not so well-protected. You've never been an opportunist, but maybe this Halloween that's about to change. Maybe life is looking up for you. Newfound friends, networking into a brand new life where you can be comfortable, loved, and happy.

After a long wait, so long you stopped checking your watch—it's your turn. The clerk smirks at you, and for a moment he looks almost sinister, but you decide that's just due to a nervous tic.

"Yes?" he says, raising one side of his hairy brow. "How may I be helping you?"

ACKNOWLEDGEMENTS

Many thanks to the following:

Vincenzo Bilof for finding the manuscript worthy and giving it a proper home.

Jess Landry for seeing the book through its final stages.

Kris Triana and Randall Lahrman for the beta notes.

Don Noble for knocking it out of the park with the gorgeous cover. Hire this man.

Kira Louise Montgomery, the strangest and the sweetest creature.

Valerie. Always.

No thank you to:

Sexy Halloween costumes. Keep Halloween scary and weird you poseurs.

ABOUT THE AUTHOR

Chad Stroup received his MFA in Fiction from San Diego State University. His dark short stories, poetry, and other whatnot have been and shall continue to be featured in various anthologies. *Secrets of the Weird*, Stroup's debut novel, is available from Grey Matter Press. Find out more about his past and upcoming work by visiting his blog Subvertbia at http://subvertbia.blogspot.com/, following him on Instagram (@chadxstroup), and/or dropping by his Facebook page at
https://www.facebook.com/ChadStroupWriter.

CPSIA information can be obtained
at www.ICGtesting.com
Printed in the USA
FSHW012307160719
60075FS